KU-489-594

Withdrawn from stock

Dublin Public Libraries

CARRYING THE GREEK'S HEIR

CARRYING THE GREEK'S HEIR

BY

SHARON KENDRICK

All rights reserved including the right of reproduction in whole or in part in any form. This edition is published by arrangement with Harlequin Books S.A.

This is a work of fiction. Names, characters, places, locations and incidents are purely fictional and bear no relationship to any real life individuals, living or dead, or to any actual places, business establishments, locations, events or incidents. Any resemblance is entirely coincidental.

This book is sold subject to the condition that it shall not, by way of trade or otherwise, be lent, resold, hired out or otherwise circulated without the prior consent of the publisher in any form of binding or cover other than that in which it is published and without a similar condition including this condition being imposed on the subsequent purchaser.

® and TM are trademarks owned and used by the trademark owner and/or its licensee. Trademarks marked with ® are registered with the United Kingdom Patent Office and/or the Office for Harmonisation in the Internal Market and in other countries.

First published in Great Britain 2015
by Mills & Boon, an imprint of Harlequin (UK) Limited,
Large Print edition 2015
Eton House, 18-24 Paradise Road,
Richmond, Surrey, TW9 1SR

© 2015 Sharon Kendrick

ISBN: 978-0-263-25661-1

Harlequin (UK) Limited's policy is to use papers that are natural, renewable and recyclable products and made from wood grown in sustainable forests. The logging and manufacturing processes conform to the legal environmental regulations of the country of origin.

Printed and bound in Great Britain
by CPI Antony Rowe, Chippenham, Wiltshire

With special thanks to Iona Grey
(Letters to the Lost) who makes
discussing characters such fun.

And to Peter Cottee for giving me
a glimpse into a businessman's mind.

CHAPTER ONE

HE WANTED HER. He wanted her so badly he could almost taste it.

Alek Sarantos felt the heavy jerk of lust as he drummed his fingers against the linen tablecloth. Tall candles flickered in the breeze and the rich perfume of roses scented the air. He shifted his position slightly but still he couldn't get comfortable.

He was…restless. More than restless.

Maybe it was the thought of returning to the crazy pace of his London life which had heightened his sexual hunger, so that it pulsed through his veins like thick, sweet honey. His throat tightened. Or maybe it was just her.

He watched as the woman walked through the long grass towards him, brushing past meadow flowers which gleamed like pale discs in the

Leabharlanna Poibli Chathair Baile Átha Cliath

Dublin City Public Libraries

dying light of the summer evening. The rising moon illuminated a body showcased by a plain white shirt, tucked into a dark skirt which looked at least a size too small. A tightly tied apron emphasised her hips. Everything about her was soft, he thought. Soft skin. Soft body. The thick hair which was plaited in a heavy rope and fell down to the middle of her back was silky soft.

His lust was insistent—his groin the opposite of soft—yet she wasn't his type. Definitely not. He didn't usually get turned on by curvy waitresses who greeted you with an uncomplicated, friendly smile. He liked his women lean and independent, not gently rounded and wholesome. Hard-eyed women who dropped their panties with ease and without question. Who took him on his terms—which had no room for manoeuvre. Terms which had helped carve out his position as a man of influence and given him a lifestyle free of domestic tie or encumbrance. Because he didn't want either. He avoided anyone he suspected might be soft, or needy or—heaven forbid—*sweet*. Sweet wasn't a quality he required in a bed partner.

So why was he lusting after someone who'd been drifting around the periphery of his vision all week, like a ripe plum waiting to fall from the tree? Something to do with her apron, perhaps— some late-onset uniform fetish, which was playing some very erotic fantasies in his head?

'Your coffee, sir.'

Even her voice was soft. He remembered hearing its low, musical cadence when she'd been comforting a child who had cut open his knee on one of the gravel paths. Alek had been returning from a game of tennis with the hotel pro when he'd seen her crouching down beside the boy, exuding a general air of unflappability. She'd stemmed the flow of blood with her handkerchief as an ashen-faced nanny had stood shaking nearby and, turning her head, had seen Alek. She'd told him to 'Go inside and get a first-aid kit' in the calmest voice he'd ever heard. And he had. A man more used to issuing orders than taking them, he'd returned with the kit and felt a savage twist of pain in his gut to see the boy looking up at her with such trust shining from his teary eyes.

She was leaning forward now as she placed the cup of coffee in front of him, drawing his attention to her breasts, which were straining tightly against her shirt. Oh, God. Her breasts. He found himself wondering what her nipples might look like if they were peaking towards his lips. As she straightened up he saw pewter-grey eyes framed by a pale and heavy fringe. She wore no adornment other than a thin gold chain around her neck and a name badge which said *Ellie.*

Ellie.

As well as being cool and unflappable towards small boys, she'd spent the week anticipating his every need—and while that was nothing new to someone like him, her presence had been surprisingly unobtrusive. She hadn't tried to engage him in conversation, or wow him with wisecracks. She'd been pleasant and friendly but hadn't hinted about her evenings off, or offered to show him around. In short, she hadn't come onto him like any other woman would have done.

She had treated him with the same quiet civility she'd exhibited towards every other guest in the discreet New Forest hotel—and maybe that's what was bugging him. His mouth hardened—for it was almost unheard of for Alek Sarantos to be treated like other people.

But it wasn't just that which had captured his interest. She had an air about her which he couldn't quite put his finger on. Ambition maybe, or just some quiet professional pride. Was it that which made his gaze linger for a heartbeat too long—or the fact that she reminded him of himself, more years ago than he cared to remember? He'd once had that same raw ambition—back in the days when he'd started out with nothing and waited tables, just like her. When money had been tight and the future uncertain. He had worked hard to escape his past and to forge a new future and had learnt plenty of lessons along the way. He'd thought that success was the answer to every problem in life, but he had been wrong. Success made the pill sweeter, but you still had to swallow the pill all the same.

Wasn't he realising that now—when he'd achieved every single thing he'd set out to achieve? When every hurdle had been leapt over and unimaginable riches were stuffed into his various bank accounts. Didn't seem to matter how much he gave away to charity, he still kept making more. And sometimes that left him with a question which made him feel uncomfortable— a question he couldn't seem to answer, but which he'd been asking himself more and more lately.

Was this all there was?

'Will there be anything else, Mr Sarantos?' she was asking him.

The waitress's voice washed over him like balm. 'I'm not sure,' he drawled and lifted his eyes to the sky. Above him, stars were spattering the darkening sky—as if some celestial artist had sprayed the canvas silver. He thought of returning to London the following day and a sudden, inexplicable yearning made him lower his head and meet her gaze. 'The night is still young,' he observed.

She gave him a quick smile. 'When you've been

waiting tables all evening, eleven-thirty doesn't really feel *young*.'

'I guess not.' He dropped a lump of sugar in his coffee. 'What time do you finish?'

Her smile wavered, as if the question wasn't one she'd been anticipating. 'In about ten minutes' time.'

Alek leant back in his chair and studied her some more. Her legs were faintly tanned and the smoothness of her skin made you almost forget how cheap her shoes were. 'Perfect,' he murmured. 'The gods must be smiling on us. So why don't you join me for a drink?'

'I can't.' She shrugged as if in answer to his raised eyebrows. 'I'm not really supposed to fraternise with customers.'

Alek gave a hard smile. Wasn't *fraternise* an old-fashioned word, which had its roots in *brotherly*? An irrelevant word as far as he was concerned, because he'd never had brothers. Never had anyone. Well, nobody that mattered, that was for sure. He'd always been alone in the world and that was the way he liked it. The way he intended to keep it. Except maybe for this starlit night, which was crying out for a little female company. 'I'm just asking you to join me for a drink, *poulaki mou*,' he said softly. 'Not to drag you off to some dark corner and have my wicked way with you.'

'Better not,' she said. 'It's against hotel policy. Sorry.'

Alek felt the stir of something unknown whispering down his spine. Was it the sensation of being refused something—no matter how small—which had started his heart racing? *How long since he had been refused anything and felt this corresponding frisson of excitement? A heady feeling that you might actually have to make an effort—instead of the outcome being entirely predictable.*

'But I'm leaving tomorrow evening,' he said.

Ellie nodded. She knew that. Everyone in the hotel did. They knew plenty about the Greek billionaire who had been creating a stir since he'd arrived at The Hog last week. As the most luxurious hotel in the south of England, they were used

to rich and demanding guests—but Alek Sarantos was richer and more demanding than most.
His personal assistant had actually sent a list of
his likes and dislikes before he'd arrived and all
the staff had been advised to study it. And even
though she'd considered it slightly over the top,
Ellie had got stuck right in, because if a job was
worth doing—it was worth doing well.

She knew he liked his eggs 'over easy' because
he'd lived in America for a while. That he drank
red wine, or sometimes whisky. His clothes had
arrived before he did—delivered by special cou-
rier and carefully wrapped in layers of filmy tis-
sue paper. There had even been a special staff
pep talk just before he'd arrived.

'Mr Sarantos must be given space,' they'd been
told. 'Under no circumstances must he be disturbed unless he shows signs of wanting to be
disturbed. It's a coup for someone like him to
stay in this hotel, so we must make him feel as if
it's his own home.'

Ellie had taken the instructions literally because
The Hog's training scheme had given her stabil-

ity and hope for the future. For someone who'd never been any good at exams, it had offered a career ladder she was determined to climb, because she wanted to make something of herself. To be strong and independent.

Which meant that, unlike every other female in the place, she had tried to regard the Greek tycoon with a certain impartiality. She hadn't attempted to flirt with him, as everyone else had been doing. She was practical enough to know her limitations and Alek Sarantos would never be interested in someone like *her*. Too curvy and too ordinary—she was never going to be the preferred choice of an international playboy, so why pretend otherwise?

But of course she had looked at him. She suspected that even a nun might have given him a second glance because men like Alek Sarantos didn't stray onto the average person's radar more than a couple of times in a lifetime.

His rugged face was too hard to be described as handsome and his sensual lips were marred by a twist of ruthlessness. His hair was ebony, his skin like polished bronze, but it was his dark-fringed eyes which captured your attention and made it difficult to look away. Unexpectedly blue eyes, which made her think of those sunlit seas you always saw in travel brochures. Sardonic eyes which seemed to have the ability to make her feel...

What?

Ellie shook her head slightly. She wasn't sure. As if she sensed something lost in him? As if, on some incomprehensible level, they were kindred spirits? Stupid crazy stuff she shouldn't be feeling, that was for sure. Her fingers tightened around the tray. It was definitely time to excuse herself and go home.

But Alek Sarantos was still staring as if he was waiting for her to change her mind and as those blue eyes seared into her she felt a brief wobble of temptation. Because it wasn't every day a Greek billionaire asked you to have a drink with him.

'It's getting on for twelve,' she said doubtfully.

'I'm perfectly capable of telling the time,' he said with a touch of impatience. 'What happens if you stay out past midnight—does your car turn into a pumpkin?'

Ellie jerked back her head in surprise. She was amazed he knew the story of Cinderella—did that mean they had the same fairy tales in Greece?—though rather less surprised that he'd associated her with the famous skivvy.

'I don't have a car,' she said. 'Just a bicycle.'

'You live out in the middle of nowhere and you don't have a car?'

'No.' She rested the tray against her hip and smiled, as if she were explaining elementary subtraction to a five-year-old. 'A bike is much more practical round here.'

'So what happens when you go to London—or the coast?'

'I don't go to London very often. And we do have such things as trains and buses, you know. It's called public transport.'

He dropped another cube of sugar in his coffee. 'I didn't use any kind of public system until I was fifteen.'

'Seriously?'

'Absolutely.' He glanced up at her. 'Not a train or a bus—not even a scheduled airline.'

She stared at him. What kind of life had he led? For a moment she was tempted to offer him a glimpse of hers. Maybe she should suggest meeting tomorrow morning and taking the bus to nearby Milmouth-on-Sea. Or catching a train somewhere—anywhere. They could drink scalding tea from paper cups as the countryside sped by—she'd bet he'd never done *that*.

Until she realised that would be overstepping the mark, big time. He was a hotshot billionaire and she was a waitress and while guests sometimes pretended to staff that they were equals, everyone knew they weren't. Rich people liked to play at being ordinary, but for them it was nothing but a game. He'd asked her to stay for a drink but, really, what possible interest could a tycoon like him have in someone like her? His unusually expansive mood might evaporate the moment she sat down. She knew he could be impatient and demanding. Didn't the staff on Reception say he'd given them hell whenever he'd lost his internet connection—even though he was supposed to be on holiday and, in her opinion, people on holiday shouldn't be working.

But then Ellie remembered something the general manager had told her when she'd first joined the hotel's training scheme. That powerful guests sometimes wanted to talk—and if they did, you should let them.

So she looked into his blue eyes and tried to ignore the little shiver of awareness which had started whispering over her skin. 'How come,' she questioned, trying to make her voice sound cool and casual, 'it took until the age of fifteen before you went on public transport?'

Alek leant back in his chair and considered her question and wondered whether now might be the right time to change the subject, no matter how easy he found it to talk to her. Because the reality of his past was something he usually kept off-limits. He had grown up in a pampered palace of a home—with every luxury known to man.

And he had hated every minute of it.

The place had been a fortress, surrounded by

high walls and snarling dogs. A place which had kept people out as well as in. The most lowly of staff were vetted before being offered employment, and paid obscenely well to turn a blind eye to his father's behaviour. Even family holidays were tainted by the old man's paranoia about security. He was haunted by the threat of stories about his lifestyle getting into the papers—terrified that anything would be allowed to tarnish his outward veneer of respectability.

Crack teams of guards were employed to keep rubber-neckers, journalists and ex-lovers at bay. Frogmen would swim silently in reconnaissance missions around foreign jetties, before their luxury yacht was given the all-clear to sail into harbour. When he was growing up, Alek didn't know what it was like not to be tailed by the shadowy presence of some burly bodyguard. And then one day he had escaped. At fifteen, he had walked away, leaving his home and his past behind and cutting his ties with them completely. He had gone from fabulous wealth to near penury but had embraced his new lifestyle with eagerness and hunger. No longer would he be tainted by his father's fortune. Everything he owned, he would earn for himself and that was exactly what he'd done. It was the one thing in life he could be proud of. His mouth hardened. Maybe the only thing.

He realised that the waitress was still waiting for an answer to his question and that she no longer seemed to be in any hurry to get off duty. He smiled, expectation making his heart beat a little faster. 'Because I grew up on a Greek island where there were no trains and few buses.'

'Sounds idyllic,' she said.

Alek's smile faded. It was such a cliché. The moment you said *Greek island*, everyone thought you were talking about paradise, because that was the image they'd been fed. But serpents lurked in paradise, didn't they? There were any number of tortured souls living in those blindingly white houses which overlooked the deep blue sea. There were all kinds of dark secrets which lay hidden at the heart of seemingly normal lives. *Hadn't he found that out, the hard way?* 'It looked very idyllic from the outside,' he said. 'But things are rarely what they seem when you dig a little deeper.'

'I suppose not,' she said. She transferred the tray to her other hand. 'And does your family still live there?'

His smile was slow—like a knife sinking into wet concrete. His *family*? That wouldn't be his word of choice to describe the people who had raised him. His father's whores had done their best, with limited success—but surely even they were better than no mother at all. Than one who'd run out on you and never cared enough to lift the phone to find out how you were.

'No,' he said. 'The island was sold after my father died.'

'A whole island?' Her lips parted. 'You mean your father actually *owned an island*?'

Another stab of lust went kicking to his groin as her lips parted. If he'd announced that he had a home on Mars, she couldn't have looked more shocked. But then, it was easy to forget how isolating wealth could be—especially to someone like her. If she didn't even own a car, then she might have trouble getting her head around someone having their own island. He glanced at her hands and, for some reason, the sight of her unmanicured nails only intensified his desire and he realised that he hadn't been entirely honest when he'd told her he wasn't planning to drag her away to a dark corner. He thought he'd like that very much.

'You've been standing there so long that you've probably come to the end of your shift,' he said drily. 'You could have had that drink with me after all.'

'I suppose I could.' Ellie hesitated. He was so persistent. Flatteringly so. She wondered why. Because he'd been almost *friendly* since he'd helped with the little boy who'd cut his knee? Or because she'd displayed a degree of reluctance to spend time with him and he wasn't used to that? Probably. She wondered what it must be like, to be Alek Sarantos—so sure of yourself that nobody ever turned you down.

'What are you so scared of?' he taunted.

'Don't you think I'm capable of behaving like a gentleman?'

It was one of those life-defining moments. Sensible Ellie would have shaken her head and said no thanks. She would have carried the tray back to the kitchen, unlocked her bike and cycled home to her room in the nearby village. But the moonlight and the powerful scent of the roses were making her feel the opposite of sensible. The last time a man had asked her on a date—and you couldn't really call this a date—was over a year ago. She'd been working such unsociable hours that there hadn't been a lot of opportunity for down time.

She looked into his eyes. 'I hadn't really thought about it.'

'Well, think about it now. You've been waiting on me all week, so why not let me wait on you for a change? I have a fridge stocked with liquor I haven't touched. If you're hungry, I can feed you chocolate or apricots.' He rose to his feet and raised his eyebrows. 'So why don't I pour you a glass of champagne?'

'Why? Are you celebrating something?'

He gave a low laugh. 'Celebration isn't man-datory. I thought all women liked champagne.'

'Not me.' She shook her head. 'The bubbles make me sneeze. And I'm cycling home—I don't want to run over some poor, unsuspecting pony who's wandered out into the middle of the road. I think I'd prefer something soft.'

'Of course you would.' He slanted her an odd kind of smile. 'Sit down and let me see what I can find.'

He went inside the self-contained villa which stood within the extensive hotel grounds and Ellie perched awkwardly on one of the cane chairs, praying nobody would see her, because she shouldn't be sitting on a guest's veranda as if she had every right to do so.

She glanced across the silent lawn, where a huge oak tree was casting an enormous shadow. The wild flowers which edged the grass swayed gently in the breeze and, in the background, lights blazed brightly from the hotel. The din-ing room was still lit with candles and she could see people lingering over coffee. In the kitchen, staff would be frantically washing up and longing to get home. Upstairs, couples would be removing complimentary chocolates from on top of the Egyptian linen pillows, before getting into bed. Or maybe they would be sampling the deep, twin baths for which The Hog was so famous.

She thought she saw something glinting from behind the oak tree and instinctively she shrank back into the shadows, but before she could work out exactly what it was—Alek had returned with a frosted glass of cola for her, and what looked like whisky, for him.

'I guess I should have put them on a tray,' he said.

She took a sip. 'And worn an apron.'

He raised his eyebrows. 'Perhaps I could borrow yours?'

The implication being that she remove her apron…Ellie put her glass down, glad that the darkness disguised her suddenly hot cheeks because the thought of removing anything was making her heart race. Suddenly, the moonlight and the roses and the glint in his eyes was making her feel way too vulnerable.

'I can't stay long,' she said quickly.

'Somehow I wasn't expecting you to. How's your cola?'

'Delicious.'

He leant back in his chair. 'So tell me why a young woman of twenty…?' He raised his eyebrows.

'I'm twenty-five,' she supplied.

'Twenty-five.' He took a sip of whisky. 'Ends up working in a place like this.'

'It's a great hotel.'

'Quiet location.'

'I like that. And it has a training scheme which is world famous.'

'But what about…' he paused '…nightlife? Clubs and boyfriends and parties? The kind of thing most twenty-five-year-olds enjoy.'

Ellie watched the bubbles fizzing around the ice cubes he'd put in her cola. Should she explain that she'd deliberately opted for a quiet life which contrasted with the chaos which had defined her childhood? Somewhere where she could concentrate on her work, because she didn't want to end up like her mother, who thought a woman's ambition should be to acquire a man who was a meal ticket. Ellie had quickly learnt how she *didn't* want to live. She was never going to trawl the internet, or hang around nightclubs. She had never owned a thigh-skimming skirt or push-up bra. She was never going to date someone just because of what they had in their wallet.

'Because I'm concentrating on my career,' she said. 'My ambition is to travel and I'm going to make that happen. One day I'm hoping to be a general manager—if not here, then in one of the group's other hotels. Competition is pretty fierce, but there's no harm in aiming high.' She sipped her cola and looked at him. 'So that's me. What about you?'

Alek swirled the whisky around in his glass. Usually he would have changed the subject, because he didn't like talking about himself. But she had a way of asking questions which made him want to answer and he still couldn't work out why.

He shrugged. 'I'm a self-made man.'

'But you said—'

'That my father owned an island? He did. But he didn't leave his money to me.' And if he had, Alek would have thrown it back in his face. He would sooner have embraced a deadly viper than taken a single drachma of the old man's fortune. He felt his gut tighten. 'Everything I own, I earned for myself.'

'And was that…difficult?'

The softness of her voice was hypnotic. It felt like balm being smoothed over a wound which had never really healed. And wasn't this what men had done since the beginning of time? Drunk a little too much whisky and then offloaded on some random woman they would never see again?

'It was a liberation,' he said truthfully. 'To cut my ties with the past.'

She nodded, as if she understood. 'And start over?'

'Exactly that. To know that every decision I make is one I can live with.'

His cell phone chose precisely that moment to start ringing and automatically he reached into his pocket, glancing at the small screen.

Work, he mouthed as he took the call.

He launched into a long torrent of Greek, before breaking into English—so that Ellie couldn't help but sit there and listen. Though if she was being honest, it was very interesting listening to a conversation, which seemed to involve some high-powered forthcoming deal with the Chinese. And then he said other stuff, too—which was even more interesting.

'I *am* taking a holiday. You know I am. I just thought it wise to check with the New York office first.' He tapped his finger impatiently against the arm of the chair. 'Okay. I take your point. *Okay.*'

He cut the connection and saw her staring at him. 'What is it?' he demanded.

She shrugged. 'It's none of my business.'

'No, I'm interested.'

She put her drink down. 'Don't you ever stop working?'

His irritated look gave way to a faint smile which seemed to tug reluctantly at the corners of his lips. 'Ironically, that's just what my assistant was saying. He said I couldn't really nag other people to take holidays if I wasn't prepared to do so myself. They've been pushing me towards this one for ages.'

'So how come you're taking business calls at this time of night?'

'It was an important call.'

'So important that it couldn't have waited until the morning?'

'Actually, yes,' he said coolly, but Alek's heart had begun beating very fast. He told himself he should be irritated with her for butting in where she wasn't wanted, yet right then he saw it as nothing but a rather disarming honesty. Was this why people went on vacation—because it took you right out of your normal environment and shook you up? In his daily life, nobody like Ellie would have got near him for long enough to deliver a damning judgement on his inability to relax. He was always surrounded by *people*— people who kept the rest of the world at arm's length.

But the protective nucleus of his business life suddenly seemed unimportant and it was as if everything was centred on the soft face in front of him. He wondered what her hair would look like if he shook it free from its ponytail and laid it over his pillow. How that soft flesh would feel beneath him as he parted her legs. He drained the last of his whisky and put the glass down, intending to walk across the veranda and take her into his arms.

But she chose that moment to push the heavy fringe away from her eyes and the jerky gesture suddenly brought him to his senses. He frowned, like someone wakening from a sleep. Had he really been planning to seduce her? He looked at the cheap shoes and unvarnished nails. At the heavy fringe, which looked as if she might trim it herself. *Was he insane?* She was much too sweet for someone like him.

'It's getting late,' he said roughly, rising to his feet. 'Where's your bike?'

She blinked at him in surprise, as if the question wasn't one she had been expecting. 'In the bike shed.'

'Come on,' he said. 'I'll walk you there.'

He could see the faint tremble of her lips as she shook her head.

'Honestly, there's no need. I see myself home every night,' she said. 'And it's probably best if I'm not seen with you.'

'I am walking you back,' he said stubbornly. 'And I won't take no for an answer.'

He could sense her disappointment as they walked over the moonlit grass and he told himself that he was doing the right thing. There were a million women who could be his for the taking—better steer clear of the sweet and sensible waitress.

They reached the hotel and she gave him an awkward smile. 'I have to go and change and fetch my bag,' she said. 'So I'd better say goodnight. Thanks for the drink.'

Alek nodded. 'Goodnight, Ellie,' he said and leant towards her, intending to give her a quick kiss on either cheek, but somehow that didn't happen.

Did she turn her head, or did he? Was that why their mouths met and melded, in a proper kiss? He saw her eyes widen. He felt the warmth of her breath. He could taste the sweetness of cola and it reminded him of a youth and an innocence which had never been his. It was purely reflex which made him pull her into his arms and deepen the kiss and her tiny gasp of pleasure was one he'd heard countless times before.

And that was all he needed. All his frustration and hunger broke free; his hands skimmed hungrily over her body as he moved her further into the shadows and pressed her up against a wall. He groaned as he felt the softness of her belly and it made him want to imprint his hardness against her. To show her just what he had and demonstrate how good it would feel if he were deep inside her. Circling his palm over one peaking nipple, he closed his eyes. Should he slip his hand beneath her uniform skirt and discover whether she was as wet as he suspected? Slide her panties down her legs and take her right here, where they stood?

The tiny moan she made in response to the increased pressure of his lips was almost enough for him to act out his erotic thoughts.

Almost, but not quite.

Reason seeped into his brain like the cold drip of a tap and he drew back, even though his body was screaming out its protest. Somehow he ignored the siren call of his senses, just as he ignored the silent plea in her eyes. Because didn't he value his reputation too much to make out with some anonymous waitress?

It was several moments before he could trust himself to speak and he shook his head in faint disbelief. 'That should never have happened.'

Ellie felt as if he'd thrown ice-cold water over her and she wondered why he had stopped. Surely he had felt it, too? That amazing chemistry. That sheer *magic*. Nobody had ever kissed her quite like that before and she wanted him to carry on doing it. And somehow her bold words tumbled out before she could stop them.

'Why not?'

There was a pause. 'Because you deserve more than I can ever offer. Because I'm the last kind of man you need. You're much too sweet and I'm nothing but a big bad wolf.'

'Surely I should be the judge of that?'

He gave a bitter smile. 'Go home, Ellie. Get out of here before I change my mind.'

Something dark came over his face—something which shut her out completely. He said something abrupt, which sounded like *'Goodbye,'* before turning his back on her and walking back over the starlit grass.

CHAPTER TWO

'WAS THAT YOUR boyfriend I saw you with last night?'

The question came out of nowhere and Ellie had to force herself to concentrate on what the guest was saying, instead of the frustrated thoughts which were circling like crows in her mind. Because of the recent heat wave, the restaurant had been fully booked and she'd been rushed off her feet all day. The lobster salad and summer pudding had sold out, and there had been a run on the cocktail of the month—an innocuous-tasting strawberry punch with a definite kick to it.

But now there was only one person left, a wafer-thin blonde who was lingering over her third glass of wine. Not that Ellie was counting. Well, actually, she was. She just wanted the woman to hurry up so that she could finish her shift in peace. Her head was pounding and she was exhausted—probably because she hadn't slept a wink last night. She'd just lain on her narrow bed, staring up at the ceiling—wide-eyed and restless and thinking about what had happened. Or rather, what hadn't happened. Telling herself that it was insane to get herself worked up about one kiss with a man who shouldn't really have been kissing her.

He was a billionaire Greek who was *way* off limits. She didn't know him, he hadn't even taken her on a date and yet... She licked her lips, which had suddenly grown very dry. Things had got pretty hot, pretty quickly, hadn't they? She could still recall his hands cupping her breasts and making them ache. She remembered wriggling with frustration as he pushed her up against the wall—his rock-hard groin pressing flagrantly against her. For a few seconds she'd thought he was going to try and have sex with her right there, and hadn't part of her wanted that? It might have been insanely wrong and completely out of character—but in the darkness of the summer night, she had wanted him more badly than she'd ever wanted anyone. She'd seen a side of herself she didn't recognise and didn't like very much. She bit her lip. A side like her *mother*?

The blonde was still looking at her with the expression of a hungry bird who had just noticed a worm wriggling up through the soil. 'So he *is* your boyfriend?' she prompted.

'No,' said Ellie quickly. 'He's not.'

'But you were kissing him.'

Nervously, Ellie's fingers slid along the frosted surface of the wine bottle before she recovered herself enough to shove it back in the ice bucket. She glanced around, terrified that another member of staff might have overheard, because although The Hog was famously laid-back and didn't have rules just for the sake of it—there was one which had been drummed into her on her very first day... And that was: you didn't get intimate with the guests.

Ever.

Awkwardly, she shrugged. 'Was I?' she questioned weakly.

The blonde's glacial eyes were alight with curiosity. 'You know you were,' she said slyly. 'I was having a cigarette behind that big tree and I spotted you. Then I saw him walk you back to the hotel—you weren't exactly being discreet.'

Briefly, Ellie closed her eyes as suddenly it all made sense. So that was the brief flare of light she'd seen from behind the tree trunk and the sense that somebody was watching them. She should have done the sensible thing and left then. 'Oh,' she said.

'Yes, *oh*. You *do* know who he is, don't you?'

Ellie stiffened as a pair of lake-blue eyes swam into her memory and her heart missed a beat. *Yes, the most gorgeous man I've ever seen. A man who made me believe all the fairy-tale stuff I never believed before.* 'Of course I do. He's... he's...'

'One of the world's richest men man who usually hangs out with supermodels and heiresses,' said the blonde impatiently. 'Which makes me wonder, what was he doing with you?'

Ellie drew back her shoulders. The woman's

line of questioning was battering her at a time when she was already feeling emotionally vulnerable, but surely she didn't have to stand here and take these snide insinuations—guest or no guest. 'I don't really see how that's relevant.'

'Don't you? But you liked him, didn't you?' The blonde smiled. 'You liked him a lot.'

'I don't kiss men I don't like,' said Ellie defensively, aware of the irony of her remark, considering it was over a year since she'd kissed *anyone*.

The blonde sipped her wine. 'You do realise he has a reputation? He's known as a man of steel, with a heart to match. Actually, he's a bit of a *bastard* where women are concerned. So what have you got to say to that...' there was a pause as she leant forward to peer at Ellie's name badge '...Ellie?'

Ellie's instinct was to tell the woman that her thoughts about Alek Sarantos were strictly confidential, but the memory of his hands moving with such sweet precision over her body was still so vivid that it was hard not to blush. Suddenly it was easy to forget that at times he'd been a demanding and difficult workaholic of a guest, with an impatience he hadn't bothered to hide.

Because now all she could think about was the way she'd responded so helplessly to him and if he hadn't pulled away and done the decent thing, there was no saying what might have happened. Well, that wasn't quite true. She had a very good idea what might have happened.

She chewed on her lip, remembering the chivalrous way he'd told her to go home and the way she'd practically begged him not to leave her. Why *shouldn't* she defend him?

'I think people may have him all wrong,' she said. 'He's a bit of a pussycat, actually.'

'A pussycat?' The blonde nearly choked on her wine. 'Are you serious?'

'Very,' said Ellie. 'He's actually very sweet— and very good company.'

'I bet he was. He'd obviously been flirting with you all week.'

'Not really,' said Ellie, her cheeks growing pink again. What was it with all this blushing? 'We'd just chatted and stuff over the week. It wasn't until...' Her voice trailed away.

'Until?'

Ellie stared into the woman's glacial eyes. It all seemed slightly unreal now. As if she'd imagined the whole thing. Like a particularly vivid dream, which started to fade the moment you woke up. 'He asked me to join him for a drink because it was his last night here.'

'And so you did?'

Ellie shrugged. 'I don't think there's a woman alive who would have turned him down,' she said truthfully. 'He's...well, he's gorgeous.'

'I'll concur with that. And a brilliant kisser, I bet?' suggested the blonde softly.

Ellie remembered the way his tongue had slipped inside her mouth and how deliciously intimate that had felt. How, for a few brief moments, she'd felt as if someone had sprinkled her with stardust. It had only been a kiss, but still... 'The best,' she said, her voice growing husky.

The blonde didn't answer for a moment and when eventually she did there was an ugly note in her voice. 'And what would you say if I told you he had a girlfriend? That she was waiting for him back in London, while he was busy making out with you?'

Ellie's initial disbelief was followed by a stab of disappointment and the dawning realisation that she'd behaved like a fool. What did she think—that someone like Alek Sarantos was free and looking to start a relationship with someone like *her*? Had she imagined that he was going to come sprinting across the hotel lawn to sweep her off her feet—still in her waitress uniform—just like in that old film which always used to make her blub? Hadn't part of her hoped he hadn't meant it when he'd said *goodbye*—and that he might come back and find her?

A wave of recrimination washed over her. Of course he wasn't coming back and *of course* he had a girlfriend. Someone beautiful and thin and rich, probably. The sort of woman who could run for a bus without wearing a bra. Did she really imagine that *she*—the much too curvy Ellie

Brooks—would be any kind of competition for someone like that?

And suddenly she felt not just stupid, but *hurt*. She tried to imagine his girlfriend's reaction if she'd seen them together. Didn't he care about loyalty or trampling over other people's feelings?

'He never said anything to me about a girl-friend.'

'Well, he wouldn't, would he?' said the blonde. 'Not in the circumstances. It's never a good move if a man mentions his lover while making out with someone else.'

'But nothing happened!'

'But you would have liked it to, wouldn't you, Ellie? From where I was standing, it looked pretty passionate.'

Ellie felt sick. She'd been a few minutes away from providing a live sex show! She wanted to walk away. To start clearing the other tables and pretend this conversation had never happened. But what if the blonde went storming into the general manager's office to tell her what she'd seen? There would be only one route they could take and that would be to fire her for unprofessional behaviour. *And she couldn't afford to lose her job and the career opportunity of a lifetime, could she? Not for one stupid kiss.*

'If I'd had any idea that he was involved with someone else, then I would never—'

'Do you often make out with the guests?'

'Never,' croaked Ellie.

'Just him, huh?' The blonde raised her brow. 'Did he say why he was keeping such a low profile?'

Ellie hesitated. She remembered the way he'd smiled at her—almost wistfully—when the little boy with the cut knee had flung his arms around her neck. She remembered how ridiculously *flattered* she'd felt when he insisted on that drink. She'd thought they'd had a special bond—when all the time he was just *using* her, as if she were one of the hotel's special offers. Angrily, her mind flitted back to what he had told her. 'He's been working day and night on some big new deal with the Chinese which is all top secret. And he said his staff had been nagging him for ages to take a vacation.'

'Really?' The blonde smiled, before dabbing at her lips with a napkin. 'Well, well. So he's human, after all. Stop looking so scared, Ellie—I'm not going to tell your boss, but I will give you a bit of advice. I'd stay away from men like Alek Sarantos in future, if I were you. Men like that could eat someone like you for breakfast.'

Alek sensed that something was amiss from the minute he walked into the boardroom but, try as he might, he couldn't quite put his finger on it. The deal went well—his deals always went well—although the Chinese delegation haggled his asking price rather more than he had been anticipating. But he pronounced himself pleased when the final figure was agreed, even if he saw a couple of members of the delegation smirking behind their files. Not a bad day's work, all told. He'd bought a company for peanuts, he'd turned it around—and had now sold it on for a more than healthy profit.

It wasn't until they all were exiting the board-room when the redhead who'd been interpret-ing for them sashayed in his direction and said, 'Hello, pussycat,' before giving a fake growl and miming a clawing action.

Alek looked at her. He'd had a thing with her last year and had even taken her to his friend Murat's place in Umbria. But it seemed she hadn't believed him when he'd told her that theirs was no more than a casual fling. When the rela-tionship had fizzled out, she'd taken it badly, as sometimes happened. The recriminatory emails had stopped and so had the phone calls, but as he met the expression in her eyes he could tell that she was still angry.

'And just what's that supposed to mean?' he questioned coolly.

She winked. 'Read the papers, tiger,' she mur-mured, before adding, 'Scraping the barrel a bit, aren't you?'

And that wasn't all. As he left the building he noticed one of the receptionists biting her lip, as if she was trying to repress a smile, and when he got back to his office he rang straight through to his male assistant.

'What's going on, Vasos?'

'With regard to…?' his assistant enquired cautiously.

'With regard to *me*!'

'Plenty of stuff in the papers about the deal with the Chinese.'

'Obviously,' Alek said impatiently. 'Anything else?'

His assistant's hesitation was illuminating. Did he hear Vasos actually *sigh*?

'I'll bring it in,' he said heavily.

Alek sat as motionless as a piece of rock as Vasos placed the article down on the desk in front of him so that he could scan the offending piece. It was an innocuous enough diary article, featuring a two-year-old library photo, which publications still delighted in using—probably because it made him look particularly forbidding.

Splashed above his unsmiling face were the words: Has Alek Sarantos Struck Gold?

His hands knuckled as he read it.

One of London's most eligible bachelors may be off the market before too long. The Midas touch billionaire, known for his love of supermodels and heiresses, was spotted in a passionate embrace with a waitress last weekend, following candlelit drinks on the terrace of his luxury New Forest hotel.

Ellie Brooks isn't Alek's usual type but the shapely waitress declared herself smitten by the workaholic tycoon, who told her he needed a vacation before his latest eye-wateringly big deal. Seems the Greek tycoon takes relaxation quite seriously!

And, according to Ellie, Alek doesn't always live up to his Man Of Steel nickname. 'He's a pussycat,' she purred.

Perhaps business associates should keep a saucer of milk at the ready in future...

Alek glanced up to see Vasos looking ill at ease, nervously running his finger along the inside of his shirt collar as he gave Alek an apologetic shrug.

'I'm sorry, boss,' he said.

'Unless you actually wrote the piece, I see no reason for you to apologise. Did they ring here first to check the facts before they went to press?' snapped Alek.

'No.' Vasos cleared his throat. 'I'm assuming they didn't need to.'

Alek glared. 'Meaning?'

Vasos looked him straight in the eye. 'They would only have printed this without verification if it were true.'

Alek crumpled the newspaper angrily before hurling it towards the bin as if it were contaminated. He watched as it bounced uselessly off the window and the fact that he had missed made him angrier still.

Yes, it was true. He had been making out with some waitress in a public place. He'd thought with his groin instead of his brain. He'd done something completely out of character and now the readers of a downmarket rag knew all about it. His famously private life wasn't so private any more, was it?

But worst of all was the realisation that he'd

taken his eye off the ball. He'd completely mis-judged her. Maybe he'd been suffering from a little temporary sunstroke. Why else would he have thought there was something special about her—or credited her with *softness* or *honesty*, when in reality she was simply on the make? The reputation he'd built up, brick by careful brick, had been compromised by some ambitious little blonde with dollar signs in her eyes.

A slow rage began to smoulder inside him. A lot of good his enforced rest had done him. All those spa treatments and massages had been for nothing if his blood pressure was now shoot-ing through the ceiling. Those solemn thera-pists telling him he must relax had been wasting their time. He must be more burnt out than he'd thought if he'd seriously thought about having sex with some little nobody like her.

His mood stayed dark for the remainder of the day, though it didn't stop him driving a particu-larly hard bargain on his latest acquisition. He would show the world that he was most definitely *not* a pussycat! He spent the day tied up with conference calls and had early evening drinks with a Greek politician who wanted his advice.

Back in his penthouse, he listened moodily to the messages which had been left on his phone and thought about how to spend the evening. Any number of beautiful women could have been his and all he had to do was call. He thought of the aristocratic faces and bony bodies which were always available to him and found himself comparing them with the curvaceous body of Ellie. The one whose face had inexplicably made him feel...

What?

As if he could trust her?

What a fool he was. A hormone-crazed, stupid fool. Hadn't he learnt his lesson a long time ago? That women were the last species on the planet who could be trusted?

He'd spent years building up a fierce but fair persona in the business world. His reputation was of someone who was tough, assertive and professional. He was known for his vision and his dependability. He despised the 'celebrity' culture and valued his privacy. He chose his friends and lovers carefully. He didn't let them get too close and nobody ever gave interviews about him. Ever. Even the redhead—supposedly broken-hearted at the time—had possessed enough sense to go away and lick her wounds in private.

But Ellie Brooks had betrayed him. A waitress he'd treated as an equal and then made the mistake of kissing had given some cheap little interview to a journalist. How much had she made? His heart pounded because he hadn't even had the pleasure of losing himself in that soft body of hers. He'd mistakenly thought she was *too sweet* and then she'd gone and sold him down the river. He'd behaved decently and honourably by sending her chastely on her way and look at all the thanks he'd got.

His mouth hardened in conjunction with the exquisite aching in his groin.

Maybe it wasn't too late to do something about that.

CHAPTER THREE

I'M SORRY, ELLIE—but we have no choice other than to let you go.

The words still resonating painfully round in her head, Ellie cycled through the thundery weather towards the staff hostel and thought about the excruciating interview she'd just had with the personnel manager of The Hog. Of *course* they'd had a choice—they'd just chosen not to take it, that was all. Surely they could have just let her lie low and all the fuss would have died down.

Negotiating her bike along the narrow road, she tried to take in what they'd just told her. She would be paid a month's salary in lieu of notice, although she would be allowed to keep her room at the hostel for another four weeks.

'We don't want to be seen as completely heartless by kicking you out on the street,' the HR woman had told her with a look of genuine regret on her face. 'If you hadn't chosen to be indiscreet with such a high-profile guest, then we might have been able to brush over the whole incident and keep you on. But as it is, I'm afraid we can't. Not after Mr Sarantos made such a blistering complaint about the question of guest confidentiality. My hands are tied—and it's a pity, Ellie, because you showed such promise.'

And Ellie had found herself nodding as she'd left the office, because, despite her shock, hadn't she agreed with pretty much every word the manager had said? She'd even felt a bit sorry for the woman who had looked so uncomfortable while terminating her employment.

She couldn't *believe* she'd been so stupid. She had behaved inappropriately with a guest and had then compounded her transgression by talking about it to a woman who had turned out to be a journalist for some low-end tabloid. A journalist! Clutching on to the handlebars with sticky palms, she stared fixedly at the road ahead.

And that had been at the root of her sacking, apparently. The fact that she had broken trust with a valued client. She had blabbed—and Alek Sarantos was *seething*. Apparently, the telephone wires had been practically smoking when he'd rung up to complain about the diary piece which had found its way into a national newspaper.

The day was heavy and overcast and she heard the distant rumble of thunder as she brought her bike to a halt outside the hostel which was home to The Hog's junior staff. Ellie locked her bike to the railings and opened the front door. Next to one of the ten individual doorbells was her name—but not for very much longer. She had a month to find somewhere new to live. A month to find herself a new job. It was a daunting prospect in the current job market and it looked as if she'd gone straight back to square one. Who would employ her now?

A louder rumble of thunder sounded ominously as she made her way along the corridor to her small room. The day was so dark that she clicked on the light and the atmosphere was so muggy that strands of her ponytail were sticking to the back of her neck. The day yawned ahead as she filled the kettle and sat down heavily on the bed to wait for it to boil.

Now what did she do?

She stared at the posters she'd hung on the walls—giant photos of Paris and New York and Athens. All those places she'd planned to visit when she was a hotshot hotelier, which was probably never going to happen now. She should have asked about a reference. She wondered if the hotel would still give her one. One which emphasised her best qualities—or would they make her sound like some kind of desperado who spent her time trying it on with wealthy guests?

Her doorbell shrilled and she gave a start, but the sense that none of this was really happening gave her renewed hope. Was it inconceivable to think that the big boss of the hotel might have overridden his HR boss's decision? Realised that it had been nothing but a foolish one-off and that she was too valuable a member of staff to lose?

Smoothing her hands over her hair, she ran

along the corridor and opened the front door—
her heart clenching with an emotion she was too
dazed to analyse when she saw who was standing there. She blinked as if she'd somehow managed to conjure up the brooding figure from her
fevered imagination. She must have done—because why else would Alek Sarantos be outside
her home?

A few giant droplets of rain had splashed onto
the blackness of his hair and his bronze skin
gleamed as if someone had spent the morning
polishing it. She'd forgotten how startlingly blue
his eyes looked, but now she could see something faintly unsettling glinting from their sapphire depths.

And even in the midst of her confusion—*why
was he here?*—she could feel her body's instinctive response to him. Her skin prickled with a
powerful recognition and her breasts began to
ache, as if realising that here was the man who
was capable of giving her so much pleasure when
he touched them. She could feel colour rushing
into her cheeks.

'Mr Sarantos,' she said, more out of habit than anything else—but the cynical twist of his lips told her that he found her words not only inappropriate, but somehow insulting.

'Oh, please,' he said softly. 'I think we know each other well enough for you to call me Alek, don't you?'

The suggestion of intimacy unnerved her even more than his presence and her fingers curled nervelessly around the door handle she was clutching for support. Now the rumble of thunder was closer and never had a sound seemed more fitting. 'What...what are you doing here?'

'No ideas?' he questioned silkily.

'To rub in the fact that you've lost me my job?'

'Oh, but I haven't,' he contradicted softly. 'You managed to do that all by yourself. Now, are you going to let me in?'

Ellie told herself she didn't have to. She could slam the door in his face and that would be that. She doubted he would batter the door down— even though he looked perfectly capable of doing it. But she was curious about what had brought him here and the rest of the day stretched in front of her like an empty void. She was going to have to start looking for a new job—she knew that. But not today.

'If you insist,' she said, turning her back on him and retracing her steps down the corridor. She could hear him closing the front door and following her. But it wasn't until he was standing in her room that she began to wonder why she had been daft enough to let him invade her space.

Because he looked all wrong here. With his towering physique and jewelled eyes, he dominated the small space like some living, breathing treasure. He seemed larger than life and twice as intimidating—like the most outrageously alpha man she had ever set eyes on. And that was making her feel uncomfortable in all kinds of ways. There was that honeyed ache deep down in her belly again and a crazy desire to kiss him. Her body's reaction was making her thoughts go haywire and her lips felt like parchment instead of flesh. She licked them, but that only made the aching worse.

The kettle was reaching its usual ear-splitting crescendo just before reaching boiling point and the great belches of steam meant that the room now resembled a sauna. Ellie could feel a trickle of sweat running down her back. Her shirt was sticking to her skin and her jeans were clinging to her thighs and once again she became horribly aware of her own body.

She cleared her throat. 'What do you want?' she said.

Alek didn't answer. Not immediately. His anger—a slow, simmering concoction of an emotion—had been momentarily eclipsed by finding himself in the kind of environment he hadn't seen in a long time.

He looked around. The room was small and clean and she had the requisite plant growing on the windowsill, but there was a whiff of institutionalisation about the place which the cheap posters couldn't quite disguise. The bed was narrower than any he'd seen in years and an unwilling flicker of desire was his reward for having allowed his concentration to focus on *that*. But he had once lived in a room like this, hadn't he? When he'd started out—much younger than she was now—he'd been given all kinds of dark and inhospitable places to sleep. He'd worked long hours for very little money in order to earn money and get a roof over his head.

He lifted his eyes to her face, remembering the powerful way his body had reacted to her the other night and trying to tell himself that it had been a momentary aberration. Because she was plain. *Ordinary.* If he'd passed her in the street, he wouldn't have given her a second glance. Her jeans weren't particularly flattering and neither was her shirt. But her eyes looked like silver and wavy strands of pale hair were escaping from her ponytail and the ends were curling, so that in the harshness of the artificial light she looked as if she were surrounded by a faint blonde halo.

A *halo*. His mouth twisted. He couldn't think of a less likely candidate for angelic status.

'You sold your story,' he accused.

'I didn't *sell* anything,' she contradicted. 'No money exchanged hands.'

'So the journalist is clairvoyant, is that what you're saying? She just guessed we were making out?'

She shook her head. 'That's not what I'm saying at all. She saw us. She was standing behind a tree having a cigarette and saw us kissing.'

'You mean it was a set-up?' he questioned, his tone flat.

'Of course it wasn't a set-up!' She glared at him. 'You think I deliberately arranged to get myself the sack? Rather a convoluted way to go about it, don't you think? I think being caught dipping your fingers in the till is the more traditional way to go.'

He raised his eyebrows in disbelief. 'So she just *happened* to be there—'

'Yes!' she interrupted angrily. 'She did. She was a guest, staying at the hotel. And the next day she cornered me in the restaurant while I was serving her and there was no way I could have avoided talking to her.'

'You still could have just said *no comment* when she started quizzing you,' he accused. 'You didn't have to gush and call me a pussycat—to damage my business reputation and any credibility I've managed to build up. You didn't have to disclose what you'd overheard when you'd clearly been *listening in to my telephone conversation*.'

'How could I help but listen in, when you broke off to take a call in front of me?'

He glared at her. 'What right did you have to repeat *any* of it?'

'And what right do you have to come here, hurling all these accusations at me?'

'You're skirting round the issue. I asked you a question, Ellie. Are you going to answer it?'

There was an odd kind of silence before eventually she spoke.

'She told me you had a girlfriend,' she said.

He raised his eyebrows. 'So you felt that gave you the right to gossip about me, knowing it might find its way into the press?'

'How could I, when I didn't know what her job was?'

'You mean you're just habitually indiscreet?'

'Or that you're just sexually incontinent?'

He sucked in an angry breath. 'As it happens, I don't have a girlfriend at the moment and if I did, then I certainly wouldn't have been making out with you. You see, I place great store on loyalty, Ellie—in fact, I value it above everything else. While you, on the other hand, don't seem to know the meaning of the word.'

Ellie was taken aback by the coldness in his eyes. She had made a mistake, yes—but it had been a genuine one. She hadn't set out to deliberately tarnish his precious reputation.

'Okay,' she conceded. 'I spoke about you when maybe I shouldn't have done and, because of that, you've managed to get me the sack. I'd say we were quits now, wouldn't you?'

He met her gaze.

'Not quite,' he said softly.

A shiver of something unknowable whispered over her skin as she stared at him. There was something unsettling in his eyes. Something distracting about the sudden tension in his hard body. She stared at him, knowing what he was planning to do and knowing it was wrong. *So why didn't she ask him to leave?*

Because she *couldn't*. She'd dreamed about just such a moment—playing it out in her mind, when it had been little more than a fantasy. She had wanted Alek Sarantos more than she had thought it possible to want anyone and that feeling hadn't changed. If anything, it had grown even stronger. She could feel herself trembling as he reached out and hauled her against him. The angry expression on his face made it seem as if he was doing something he didn't really want to do and she felt a brief flicker of rebellion. How dare he look that way? She told herself to pull away, but the need to have him kiss her again was dominating every other consideration. And maybe this was inevitable—like the thunder which had been rumbling all day through the heavy sky. Sooner or later you just knew the storm was going to break.

His mouth came down on hers—hard—and the hands which should have been pushing him away were gripping his shoulder, as she kissed him back—just as hard. It felt like heaven and it felt like hell. She wanted to hurt him for making her lose her job. She wanted him to take back all those horrible accusations he'd made. And she wanted him to take away this terrible aching deep inside her.

Alek shuddered as he heard the little moan she made and he told himself to tug her jeans down and just *do* it. To give into what they both wanted and feed this damned hunger so that it would go away and leave him. Or maybe he should just turn around and walk out of that door and go find someone else. Someone immaculate and cool— not someone all hot and untidy from cycling on the hottest day of the year.

But she was soft in his arms. So unbelievably soft. She was like Turkish Delight when you pressed your finger against it, anticipating that first sweet, delicious mouthful. He pulled his lips away from hers and slowly raised his head, meeting a gaze which gleamed silver.

'I want you,' he said.

He saw her lips tremble as they opened, as if she was about to list every reason why he couldn't have her and he guessed there might be quite a long list. And then he saw something change—the moment when her eyes darkened and her skin started to flush. The *what-the-hell?* moment as she looked at him with naked invitation in her eyes.

'And I want you, too,' she said.

It was like dynamite. Like nothing he'd ever known as he drove his lips back down on hers. A kiss which made him feel almost savage with need. It went on and on until they were both breathless, until he drew his mouth away from hers and could suck in a ragged breath of air. Her eyes were wide and very dark and her lips were trembling. With a sense of being slightly out of control, he tugged open her shirt to reveal the spill of her breasts and stared at them in disbelief.

'*Theo,*' he said softly. 'Your breasts are magnificent.'

'A-are they?'

'They are everything I dreamed they would be. And more.'

'Have you been dreaming about my breasts?'

'Every night.'

He drew a finger over one generous curve and he heard her moan as he bent to touch his lips to the same spot. And that was when she chose to press her palm over the tight curve of his denim-covered buttock, as if tacitly giving him her permission to continue.

He groaned as he straightened up to kiss her again and once he'd started he couldn't seem to stop. It was only when she began to writhe frustratedly that he tugged off the elastic band so that her pale hair spilled free, and suddenly she managed to look both wholesome and wanton. She looked…like a *woman*, he thought longingly. Soft and curving; warm and giving.

His hands were shaking as he stripped her bare, then laid her down on the narrow bed as he removed his own clothes, his eyes not leaving her face. With shaking hands he groped for his wallet and found a condom. Thank God. Slipping it on as clumsily as if it had been his first time, he moved over her, smoothing back her thick hair with hands which were still unsteady. And as he entered her a savage cry was torn from his throat.

He moved inside her and it felt pretty close to heaven. Sweet heaven. He had to keep thinking about random stuff about mergers and acquisitions to stop himself from coming and it seemed like an eternity until at last her body began to tense beneath him. Until she stiffened and her back arched and, inexplicably—she started to cry.

Only then did Alek let go himself, although the salty wetness of her tears against his cheek gave him a moment of disquiet. Outside, the thunder seemed to split the sky. The rain began to teem down against the window. And his body was torn apart by the longest orgasm of his life.

CHAPTER FOUR

ELLIE TURNED THE sign to Closed and started
clearing away stray currants and dollops of frost-
ing from the glass counters which lined the cake
shop. She stacked cardboard boxes, swept the
floor and took off her frilly apron.

And then she went and stood at the back of the
little store, and wept.

The tears came swiftly and heavily and she
tried to think of them as cathartic as she covered her face with her hands. But as they dripped
through her fingers all she could think was: *How
had this happened? How had her life suddenly
become a living nightmare?*

She knew she'd been lucky finding work and
accommodation at Candy's Cupcakes so soon
after leaving the hotel. She'd been doubly lucky
that the kindly Bridget Brody had taken a shine

to her, and not cared about her ignominious sacking. But it was hard to focus on gratitude right now. In fact, it was hard to focus on anything except the one thing she couldn't keep ignoring. *But you couldn't make something go away, just because you wanted it to—no matter how hard you wished it would.* Her feet were heavy as she made her way up to the small, furnished apartment above the shop, but not nearly as heavy as her heart.

The mirror in the sitting room was hung in a position you couldn't avoid, unless you walked into the room with your eyes shut, which was never a good idea with such uneven floorboards. The healthy tan she'd acquired while working in the garden restaurant of The Hog had long since faded. Her face was pasty, her breasts were swollen and her skin seemed too loose for her body. And she'd lost weight. She couldn't eat anything before midday because she kept throwing up. She hadn't needed to see the double blue stripes on the little plastic stick to confirm what she already knew.

That she was pregnant with Alek Sarantos's baby and didn't know what she was going to do about it.

Slumping down in one of the overstuffed armchairs, she stared blankly into space. Actually, that wasn't quite true. There was only one thing she *could* do. She had to tell him.

She had to.

It didn't matter what her personal feelings were, or that fact that there had been a deafening silence ever since the Greek billionaire had walked out of her bedroom, leaving her naked in bed. This was about more than *her*. She knew what it was like not to have a father and no real identity. To feel invisible—as if she were only half a person. And that wasn't going to happen to her baby. She hugged her arms tightly around her chest. *She wouldn't allow it to happen.*

But how did you tell someone you were having his baby when he had withdrawn from you in more ways than one as soon as he'd had his orgasm?

Her mind drifted back to that awful moment

when she'd opened her eyes to find Alek Sarantos lying on top of her in the narrow bed in the
staff hostel. His warm skin had been sticking to
hers and his breathing sounded as if he'd been in
a race. On a purely physical level, her own body
was glowing with the aftermath of the most incredible sexual experience of her life—although
she didn't exactly have a lot to compare it with.
Her body felt as if she were floating and she
wanted to stay exactly where she was—to capture and hold on to the moment, so that it would
never end.

But unfortunately, life wasn't like that.

She wasn't sure what changed everything. They
were lying there so close and so quiet while the
rain bashed hard against the windows. It felt as
if their entire lives were cocooned in that little
room. She could feel the slowing beat of his heart
and the warmth of his breath as it fanned against
the side of her neck. She wanted to fizz over with
sheer joy. She'd had a relationship before—of
course she had—but she had never known such
a feeling of completeness. Did he feel it, too?

She remembered reaching up to whisper her fingertips over his hair with soft and rhythmical strokes. And that was the moment when she read something unmistakable on his face. The sense that he'd just made the biggest mistake of his life. She could see it in his eyes—those compelling blue eyes, which went from smoky satisfaction through to ice-cold disbelief as he realised just where he was. And with whom.

With a wince he didn't even bother disguising, he carefully eased himself away from her, making sure the condom was still intact as he withdrew. She remembered the burning of her cheeks and feeling completely out of her depth. Her mind was racing as she thought how best to handle the situation, but her experience of men was scant and of Greek billionaires, even scanter. She decided that coolness would be the way to go. She needed to reassure him that she wasn't fantasising about walking up the aisle wearing a big white dress, just because they'd had sex. To act as if making love to a man who was little more than a stranger was no big deal.

She reminded herself that what they'd done had been driven by anger and perhaps it might have been better if it had stayed that way. Because if it hadn't suddenly morphed into a disconcerting whoosh of passion, then she might not be lying there wishing he would stay and never leave. She might not be starting to understand her own mother a bit more and to wonder if this was what *she* had felt. Had she lain beside her married lover like this, and lost a little bit of her heart to him, even though she must have known that he was the wrong man?

She remembered feigning sleepiness. Letting her lashes flutter down over her eyes as if the lids were too heavy to stay open. She could hear him moving around as he picked up his clothes from the floor and began pulling them on and she risked a little peep from between her lashes, to find him looking anywhere except at her. As if he couldn't bear to look at her. But she guessed it was a measure of how skewed her thinking was that she was still prepared to give him the benefit of the doubt.

'Alek?' she said—casual enough to let him know she wouldn't mind seeing him again, but not so friendly that it could be interpreted as pushy.

He was fully dressed by now—although he looked dishevelled. It was strange to see the powerful billionaire in *her* room, his shirt all creased from where it had been lying on the floor. He was running his fingers through his ruffled hair and his skin gleamed with the exertion of sex, but it was his eyes which got to her. His eyes were cold. Cold as ice. She saw him checking in his pocket for his car keys. Or maybe he was just checking that his wallet was safe.

'That was amazing,' he said, and her suddenly happy heart wanted to burst out of her chest, until his next words killed the dream for ever.

'But a mistake,' he finished with a quick, careful smile. 'I think we both realise that. Goodbye, Ellie.'

And then he was gone and Ellie was left feeling like a fool. He didn't even slam the door and for some reason that only added to her humiliation. As if the quiet click as he shut it behind him was all he could be bothered with.

She didn't move for ages. She lay in that rumpled bed watching the rain running in rivulets over the window, like giant tears. Why had she cried afterwards? Because it had been so perfect? And that was the most stupid thing of all. It *had*. It had felt like everything her faintly cynical self had never believed in. He'd made her feel stuff she'd never felt before. As if she was gorgeous. Precious. Beautiful. Did he do that with everyone woman he had sex with? *Of course he did.* It was like tennis, or playing poker. If you practised something often enough, you got very accomplished at doing it.

She went straight to shower in the shared bathroom along the corridor in an attempt to wash away her memories, but it wasn't that easy. Vivid images of Alek seemed to have stamped themselves indelibly on her mind. She found herself thinking about him at inconvenient times of the day and night and remembering the way he had touched her. And although time would probably have faded those memories away she'd never had a chance to find out because her period had been late.

What was she talking about? Her period hadn't been *late*. It just hadn't arrived and she was normally as regular as clockwork. Waves of nausea had begun striking her at the most inopportune times and she knew she couldn't keep putting it off.

She was going to have to tell him. Not next week, nor next month—but now.

Firing her ancient computer into life, she tapped in the name of the Sarantos organisation, which seemed to have offices all over the world. She prayed he was still in London and as the distinctive blue logo flashed up on the screen, it seemed he was. According to the company website, he'd given a speech about 'Acquisitions & Mergers' at some high-profile City conference, just the evening before.

Even if she'd known his home address—which of course she didn't—it made much more sense to go to his office. She remembered him telling her that he always stayed late. She would go there and explain that she had something of vital importance to tell him and—even if it was only curiosity—she was certain he would listen.

And if he didn't?

Then her conscience would be clear, because at least she would have tried.

Wednesday was her day off and she travelled by train to London, on another of the sticky and humid days which had been dominating the English summer. Her best cotton dress felt like a rag by the time she left the train at Waterloo and she had a nightmare journey on the Underground before emerging close to St Paul's cathedral.

She found the Sarantos building without too much difficulty—a giant steel and glass monolith soaring up into the cloudless blue sky. Lots of people were emerging from the revolving doors and Ellie shrank into the shadows as she watched them heading for the local bars and Tube. How did the women manage to look so cool in this sweltering heat, she wondered—and how could they walk so quickly on those skyscraper heels they all seemed to wear?

She walked into the reception area, where the blessed cool of the air conditioning hit her like a welcome fan. She could see a sleek woman behind the desk staring at her, but she brazened it out and walked over to one of the squidgy leather sofas which were grouped in the far corner of the lobby, sinking down onto it with a feeling of relief.

A security guard she hadn't seen until that moment walked over to her.

'Can I help you, miss?'

Ellie pushed her fringe out of her eyes and forced a smile. 'I'm just waiting for my...friend.'

'And your friend's name is?'

Did she dare? And yet, wasn't the reality that in her belly was growing a son or daughter who might one day be the boss of this mighty corporation? She sucked in a deep breath, telling herself that she had every right to be here.

'His name is Alek Sarantos,' she blurted out,

but not before she had seen a wary look entering the guard's eyes.

To his credit—and Ellie's surprise—he didn't offer any judgement or try to move her on, he simply nodded.

'I'll let his office know you're here,' he said, and started to walk towards the reception desk.

He's going to tell him, thought Ellie as the reality of her situation hit her. *He's going to ring up to Alek's office and say that some mad, overheated woman is waiting downstairs for him in Reception.* It wasn't too late to make a run for it. She could be gone by the time Alek got down here. She could go back to the New Forest and carry on working for the owner of Candy's Cupcakes—who wasn't called Candy at all—and somehow scrape by, doing the best she could for her baby.

But that wasn't good enough, was it? She didn't want to bring up a child who had to *make do*. She didn't want to have to shop at thrift stores or learn a hundred ways to be inventive with a packet of lentils. She wanted her child to thrive. To have new shoes whenever he or she needed them and not have to worry about whether there was enough money to pay the rent. Because she knew how miserable that could be.

'Ellie?'

A deep Greek accent broke into her thoughts and Ellie looked up to see Alek Sarantos directly in front of her with the guard a few protective steps away. There was a note of surprise in the way he said her name, and a distinct note of unfriendliness, too.

She supposed she ought to get to her feet. To do something rather than just sit there, like a sack of potatoes which had been dumped. She licked her lips and tried to smile, but a smile was stubbornly refusing to come. And wasn't it crazy that she could look at someone who was glaring at her and *still* want him? Hadn't her body already betrayed her once, without now shamefully prickling with excited recognition—even though she'd never seen him looking quite so intimidating in an immaculately cut business suit?

Keep calm, she told herself. *Act like a grown-up.*

'Hello, Alek,' she said, even managing what she hoped was a friendly smile.

He didn't react. His blue eyes were cool. No. Cool was the wrong temperature. Icy would be more accurate.

'What are you doing here?' he questioned, almost pleasantly—but it didn't quite conceal the undertone of steel in his voice and she could see the guard stiffen, as if anticipating that some unpleasantness was about to reveal itself.

She wondered what would happen if she just came out and said it. *I'm having your baby. You're going to be a daddy, Alek!* That would certainly wipe that cold look from his face! But something stopped her. Something which felt like self-preservation. And pride. She couldn't afford to just *react*—she had to *think*. Not just for herself, but for her baby. In his eyes she'd already betrayed him to the journalist and that had made him go ballistic. She couldn't tell him about impending fatherhood when there was a brick-house of a guard standing there, flexing his muscles. She ought to give him the opportunity to hear the news in private. She owed him that much.

She kept her gaze and her voice steady—though that wasn't particularly easy in the light of that forbidding blue stare. 'I'd prefer to talk to you in private, if you don't mind.'

Alek felt a sudden darkness envelop his heart as the expression on her face told him everything. He tried to tell himself that it was the shock of finding her here which had sent his thoughts haywire, but he knew that wasn't true. Because he'd thought about her. Of course he had. He'd even wondered idly about seeing her again—and why wouldn't he? Why wouldn't he want a repeat of what had been the best sex he could remember? If only it had been that straightforward, but life rarely was.

He remembered the way he'd lain there afterwards, with his head cradled on her shoulder as he drifted in and out of a dreamy sleep. And her fingers—her soft fingers—had been stroking his hair. It had felt soothing and strangely intimate. It had kick-started something unknown inside him—something threatening enough to freak him out. He had felt the walls closing in on him—just as they were closing in on him right now.

He tried to tell himself that maybe he was mistaken—that it couldn't possibly be what he most feared. But what else could it be? No woman in her situation would turn up like this and be so unflappable when challenged—not unless she had a trump card to play. Not when he'd left her without so much as a kiss or a promise to call her again. Somehow he sensed that Ellie had more pride than to come here begging him to see her again. She'd been strong, hadn't she? An equal in his arms and out of them, despite the disparity of their individual circumstances.

He noted the shadows on her face, which suddenly seemed as grey as her eyes, and thought how *drained* she looked. His mouth tightened and a flare of anger and self-recrimination flooded through him. He was going to have to listen to her. He needed to hear what she had to say. *To find out whether what he dreaded was true.*

His mind raced. He thought about taking her to a nearby coffee shop. No. Much too public. Should he take her upstairs to his office? That might be easier. Easier to get rid of her afterwards than if he took her home. And he had no desire to take her home. He just wanted her out of his life. To forget that he'd ever met her. 'You'd better come up to my office.'

'Okay,' she said, her voice sounding brittle.

It felt bizarre to ride up in the elevator in silence but he didn't want to open any kind of discussion in such a confined space, and she seemed to feel the same. When the doors opened she followed him through the outer office and he looked across at Vasos.

'Hold all my calls,' he said—catching the flicker of surprise in his assistant's eyes.

'Yes, boss.'

Soon they were in his cool suite of offices, which overlooked the city skyline, and he thought how out of place she looked, with her flower-sprigged cotton dress and pale legs. And yet despite a face which was almost bare of make-up and the fact that her hair was hanging down her back in that thick ponytail—there was still something about her which made his body tense with a primitive recognition he didn't understand. Even though she looked pasty and had obviously lost weight, part of him still wanted to pin her down against that leather couch, which stood in the corner, and to lose himself deep inside her honey-eyed softness. His mouth flattened.

'Sit down,' he said.

'There's no need.' She hesitated, like a guest who had turned up at the wrong party and wasn't quite sure how to explain herself to the host. 'You probably want to know why I've turned up like this—'

'I know exactly why.' Never had it been more of an ordeal to keep his voice steady, but he knew that psychologically it was better to tell than to be told. To remain in control. His words came out calmly, belying the sudden flare of fear deep in his gut. 'You're pregnant, aren't you?'

She swayed. She actually swayed—reaching out to grab the edge of his desk. And despite his anger, Alek strode across the office and took hold of her shoulders and he could feel his fingers sinking into her soft flesh as he levered her down onto a chair.

'Sit down,' he repeated.

Her voice was wobbly. 'I don't want to sit down.'

'And I don't want the responsibility of you passing out on the floor of my office,' he snapped. But he pulled his hands away from her—as if continuing to touch her might risk him behaving like the biggest of all fools for a second time. He didn't want the responsibility of her, full stop. He wanted her to be nothing but a fast-fading memory of an interlude he'd rather forget—but that wasn't going to happen. Not now. Raising his voice, he called for his assistant. 'Vasos!'

Vasos appeared at the door immediately—unable to hide his look of surprise as he saw his boss leaning over the woman who was sitting slumped on a chair.

'Get me some water.' Alek spoke in Greek. 'Quickly.'

The assistant returned seconds later with a

glass, his eyes still curious. 'Will there be anything else, boss?'

'Nothing else.' Alek took the water from him. 'Just leave us. And hold all my calls.'

As Vasos closed the door behind him Alek held the glass to her lips. Her eyes were suspicious and her body tense. She reminded him of a stray kitten he'd once brought into the house as a child. The animal had been a flea-ridden bag of bones and Alek had painstakingly brought it back to full and gleaming health. It had been something he'd felt proud of. Something in that cold mausoleum of a house for him to care about. And then his father had discovered it, and…and…

His throat suddenly felt as if it had nails in it. *Why remember something like that now?* 'Drink it,' he said harshly. 'It isn't poison.'

She raised her eyes to his and the suspicion in them had been replaced by a flicker of defiance.

'But you'd probably like it to be,' she answered quietly.

He didn't answer—he didn't trust himself to. He blocked out the maelstrom of emotions which seemed to be hovering like dark spectres and waited until a little colour had returned to her cheeks. Then he walked over to his desk and put the glass down, before positioning himself in front of the vast expanse of window, his arms crossed.

'You'd better start explaining,' he said.

Ellie stared up at him. The water had restored some of her strength, but one glance at the angry sizzle from his blue eyes was enough to remind her that she was here on a mission. She wasn't trying to win friends or influence people, or because she hoped for a repeat of the passion which had got her into this situation in the first place. *So keep emotion out of it*, she told herself fiercely. *Keep to the plain and brutal facts and then you can deal with them.*

'There isn't really a lot to explain. I'm having a baby.'

'We used a condom,' he iced back. 'You know we did.'

Stupidly, that made her blush. As if discussing contraception in his place of work was hopelessly

inappropriate. But while it might be inappropriate, it was also *necessary*, she reminded herself
grimly. And she was not going to let him intimi-
date her. It had taken two of them to get into this
situation—therefore they both needed to accept
responsibility.

'I also know that condoms aren't one hundred
per cent reliable,' she said.

'So. You're an expert, are you?' He looked at
her with distaste. 'Perhaps there are other men to
whom you've taken this tale of woe. How many
more in the running, I wonder—could you tell
me my position on the list, just so I know?'

Ellie clenched her fists as a wave of fury
washed over her. She didn't *need* this—not in any
circumstances but especially not now. She made
to rise to her feet, but her legs were stubbornly
refusing to obey her brain. And even though at
that moment she wanted to run out of there and
never return, she knew that flight was an indul-
gence she simply couldn't afford.

'There's nobody else in the running,' she spat
out. 'Maybe you're different, but I don't have

sex with more than one person at the same time. So why don't you keep your unfounded accusations to yourself? I didn't come here to be your punchbag!'

'No? Then what did you come for?' The brief savagery of his dark features realigned themselves into a quizzical expression. 'Is it money you want?'

'Money?'

'That's what I said.'

Ellie's anger intensified but somehow that seemed to help, because it was giving her focus. It was making her want to fight. Not for herself, but for the tiny life growing inside her. Because *that* was what was important. *That* was the reason she had come here today, even though she'd known it was going to be an ordeal. *So think before you answer. Don't make cheap retorts just for the sake of trying to score points. Show him you mean business. Because you* do.

'I'm here to give you the facts,' she said. 'Because I thought it was your right to have them.

That you needed to be aware that there were consequences to what happened that afternoon.'

'A little dramatic, isn't it? Just turning up here like this. Couldn't you have called first to warn me?'

'You think I should have done that? Really?' She tipped her head to one side and looked at him. 'I didn't have your number because you deliberately didn't give it to me, but even if I'd managed to get hold of it—would you have spoken to me? I don't think so.'

Alek considered her words. No, he probably wouldn't, despite his faintly irrational desire to see her again. Through Vasos, he would have demanded she put everything down in an email. He would have kept her at an emotional distance, as he did with all women. But he was beginning to realise that the whys and wherefores of what had happened between them were irrelevant. Didn't matter that she'd broken a cardinal rule and invaded his workspace. There was only one thing which mattered and that was what she had just told him.

And this was one reality he couldn't just walk away from. He asked the question as if he were following some ancient male-female rule book, but if his question sounded lifeless it was because deep down he knew the answer. 'How do I know it's mine?'

'You think I'd be here if it wasn't? That I'd be putting myself through this kind of aggravation if it was someone else's baby?'

He tried telling himself that she might be calling his bluff and that he could demand a DNA test, which would have to wait until the child was born. And yet, once again something told him that no such test would be needed, and he wasn't sure why. Was it the certainty on her pale face which told him that he was the father of her child, or something more subtly complex, which defied all logic? He could hear the door of the prison swinging shut and the sound of the key being turned. He was trapped. Again. And it was the worst feeling in the world. He remembered that distant fortress and his voice sounded gritty.

Like it was coming from a long way away. 'What do you want from me?'

There was a pause as those shadowed grey eyes met his.

'I want you to marry me,' she said.

CHAPTER FIVE

WITH NARROWED EYES, Alek looked at her. 'Or what?' he questioned with soft venom. 'Marry you or you'll run blabbing to your journalist friend again? This would be a real scoop, wouldn't it? Pregnant With the Greek's Child.'

Meeting the accusation on his face, Ellie tried to stay calm. She hadn't meant to blurt it out like that—in fact, she hadn't really been planning to say that at all. She had meant to tell him that she was planning to have the baby and would respect whatever decision he made about his own involvement. She had intended to imply that she wasn't bothered one way or another—and she certainly wasn't intending to control or manipulate what was happening.

But something had happened to her during the awkward conversation which had just taken place in the alien surroundings of his penthouse office. With the air-conditioning freezing tiny beads of sweat to her forehead and her cotton dress clinging to her like a dishcloth she had felt worse than ugly. Surrounded by the unbelievable wealth of Alek's penthouse office suite, she had felt *invisible*.

She thought about all the women she'd seen leaving the building—clipping along in their high-heeled shoes with not a hair out of place. Those were the kind of women he dealt with on a daily basis, with their air of purpose and their slim, toned figures. Where did she fit into that world, with her cheap dress and a growing belly and a feeling that she had no real place of her own?

Because she didn't have any real place of her own. This was *his* world and neither she nor her baby belonged in it. How long before he conveniently forgot he had sired a child in a moment of ill-thought-out passion? How long before he married someone classy and had legitimate children who would inherit everything he owned, while her own child shrank into the shadows, forgotten and overlooked? Didn't she know better than anyone that unwanted children usually stayed that way? *She knew what it was like to be rejected by her own father.*

And that was her light-bulb moment. The moment when she knew exactly what she was going to ask for. Her ego didn't matter and neither did her pride, because this was more important than both those things. *This was for her baby.*

'I'm not threatening to blackmail you,' she said quietly. 'I've told you until I was blue in the face that the whole journalist thing was a stupid mistake, which I don't intend on repeating. I just want you to marry me, that's all.'

'That's all?' he echoed with a cruel replica of a smile. 'Why?'

'Because you're so charming, of course,' she snapped. 'And so thoughtful and—'

'Why?' he repeated, a note of steel entering his voice—as if he suspected that behind her flippancy she was teetering perilously on the brink of hysteria.

'Isn't it obvious?' With an effort she kept her gaze steady, but inside her heart was pounding so loudly she was certain he must be able to hear it. 'Because I want my baby to have some kind of security.'

'Which doesn't need to involve marriage,' he said coldly. 'If the baby really is mine, then I will accept responsibility. I can give you money. A house.' He shrugged. 'Some baubles for yourself, if that's what you're angling for.'

Baubles? *Baubles?* Did he really think her so shallow that he thought jewels might be her motivation? 'It isn't,' she said, her cheeks growing pink, 'just about the money.'

'Really? Woman claims money isn't her sole motivation.' He gave a cynical laugh. 'Wow! That must be a first. So if it isn't about the money—then what *is* it about?'

Distractedly, she rubbed at her forehead. 'I want him—or her—to know who they are—to have a real identity. I want them to bear their father's name.'

She saw the darkness which passed over his face like a cloud crossing the sun.

'And I might not have the kind of name you would want to associate with your baby,' he said harshly.

'What's that supposed to mean?'

But Alek shook his head as the old familiar shutters came slamming down—effectively sealing him off from her questions. Because marriage was a no-no for him—right at the very top of things he was never going to do. And although he'd shaken off his past a long time ago— he could never entirely escape its long tentacles. They reached out and whipped him when he wasn't expecting it. In the darkness of the night they sometimes slithered over his skin, reminding him of things he'd rather forget.

His parents' marriage had been the dark canker at the heart of his life, whose poison had spilled over into so many places. The union between a cruel man and a woman he despised so much that he couldn't even bear to say her name. His mouth hardened. Why the hell would *he* ever want to marry?

Alek's success had been public, but he'd managed to keep his life private. He had locked himself within an emotional shell in order to protect himself and he rarely let anyone get close. And hadn't that been another reason for his anger with Ellie? Not just because her indiscretion had tarnished his hard-won business reputation, but because she'd broken his foolishly misplaced trust in her.

'Maybe I'm not great husband material,' he told her. 'Ask any of the women I've dated and I'm sure they'd be happy to list all my failings. I'm selfish. I'm intolerant. I work too hard and have a low boredom threshold—especially where women are concerned.' He raised his eyebrows. 'Shall I continue?'

She shook her head, so that her ponytail swung from side to side. 'I'm not talking about a real marriage. I'm talking about a legal contract with a finite time limit.'

His eyes narrowed. 'Because?'

'Because I don't want my baby to be born illegitimate—I'm illegitimate myself. But neither do I want to spend the rest of my life with someone who doesn't even seem to like me. I'm not a complete masochist—'

'Just a partial one?' he put in mockingly.

'I must have been,' she said bitterly, 'to have had sex with you.'

'Pretty amazing sex, though,' he said, almost as an aside.

Deliberately, Ellie pushed that thought away, even though just the mention of it was enough to start her body tingling. Yes, it had been amazing. It had started out in anger but it had turned into something else. Something passionate and all consuming, which had completely blown her away. Had he felt it, too—that incredible connection? Or was she doing that thing women were so good at doing? Believing something to be true because you *wanted* it to be true.

'It doesn't matter now what the sex was like,' she said slowly. 'Because the only thing that matters now is the baby.'

He flinched as she said the word. She could see his jaw harden so that it looked as if it were carved from granite.

'Cut to the chase and tell me exactly what you're proposing,' he said.

The combination of heat, emotion and a lack of food was making her feel dizzy but Ellie knew she mustn't crumple now. The thought of having Alek in her life didn't exactly make her want to jump for joy—but it was still better than going it alone.

'We have a small wedding,' she said. 'No doubt your lawyers will want to draw up some kind of contract and that's fine by me.'

'Good of you,' he said sardonically.

'We don't even have to live together,' she continued. 'You just acknowledge paternity and provide support for the future. The baby gets your name and a share of your inheritance.' She shrugged, because the words sounded so bizarre. A few short weeks ago she'd been thinking no further than her next promotion and here she was talking about *paternity*. 'And after the birth, we can get ourselves a no-blame divorce. I think that's fair.'

'*Fair?*' He gave a short laugh. 'You mean I'm to play the tame benefactor? Sitting on the sidelines, just doling out money?'

'I'm not intending to be greedy.'

He narrowed his eyes. 'And you don't think people are going to be suspicious? To wonder why we aren't living together and why I haven't spent any time with the mother of my baby?'

'Given the way you've reacted to the news, I was assuming that being given a get-out clause would be your dream scenario.'

'Well, don't,' he snapped. 'Don't ever *assume* anything about me, Ellie. That was the first mistake you made. I am not a "pussycat" as you seem to think, not by any stretch of the imagination.'

'Don't worry. I've changed my mind about that!'

'I'm pleased to hear it.' His gaze raked over her, lingering almost reluctantly on her belly. 'I didn't plan a baby and I certainly didn't want marriage. But if these are the cards fate has dealt me—then these are the cards I'm going to have to play. And I play to win.'

She pushed her fringe out of her eyes. 'Is that supposed to be a threat?'

'Not a threat, no. But you haven't yet heard my side of the bargain.' Alek stared at her mutinous face. He knew what he had to do. No matter how much it flew in the face of everything he believed in, he was going to have to make sacrifices for his child in a way nobody had ever done for him. He was going to have to marry her. Because it was far better to have her by his side as his wife, than to leave her free to behave like a loose cannon, with his child helpless and without his protection.

His heart clenched. 'If you want my ring on your finger, then you're going to have to act like a wife,' he said. 'You will live with me—'

'I told you that wasn't—'

'I don't care what you told me,' he interrupted impatiently. 'If we're going to do this, we're going to do it properly. I want this wedding to mimic all the traditions of what a wedding should be.'

'M-mimic?' she echoed, in confusion. 'What do you mean?'

'Can't you guess?' His mouth twisted into a bitter smile. 'We will pretend. You will wear a white dress and look deep into my eyes and play the part of my adoring bride. Do you think you can manage that, Ellie?'

Ellie's stomach began to rumble and she wondered if he could hear it in the strange silence which had descended. It seemed a long time since she'd eaten that apple on the train. In fact, it seemed a long time since she'd done anything which felt remotely *normal*. One minute she'd been waiting tables and the next she was standing discussing marriage with a cold-eyed billionaire who was telling her to pretend to care about him. Suddenly she felt like a feather which had found itself bouncing around on a jet stream.

'You want to make it into some sort of farce,' she breathed.

'Not a farce. Just a performance credible

enough to convince the outside world that we have fallen in love.'

'But why?' she questioned. 'Why not just treat it like the contract we both know it is?'

He flexed his fingers and she saw the whitening of his knuckles through the deep olive skin.

'Because I want my child to have *memories*,' he said harshly. 'To be able to look at photos of their mother and father on their wedding day, and even if they are no longer together—which obviously, we won't be—then at least there will be the consolation that once we were an item.'

'But that's...that's a lie!'

'Or just illusionary?' he questioned bitterly. 'Isn't that what life is? An illusion? People see what others want them to see. And I don't want my child hurt. Let him believe that once his parents loved one another.'

Ellie watched his face become ravaged by a pain he couldn't hide. It clouded the brilliance of his blue eyes and darkened his features into a rugged mask. And despite everything, she wanted to reach out and ask him what had caused him a hurt so palpable that just witnessing it seemed intrusive. She wanted to put her arms around him and cradle him.

But he looked so remote in his beautifully cut suit, with its dark fabric moulding his powerful limbs and the white shirt collar which contrasted against his gleaming skin. He looked so proud and patrician that he seemed almost *untouchable*, which was pretty ironic when you thought about it. She cleared her throat. 'And when should this *marriage* take place?'

'I think as soon as possible, don't you? There's something a little in your face about a bride who is so *obviously* pregnant. I'll have my lawyers draw up a contract and you will move into my London apartment. We can discuss buying you a property after the birth.'

Ellie felt as if her old life was already fading. As if she'd been plucked from obscurity and placed in the spotlight of Alek's glamorous existence and she was suddenly beginning to realise just how powerful that spotlight could be. But when she stopped to think about it, what did she imagine would happen next? That she'd carry on selling cupcakes while wearing his ring on her finger? 'I suppose so,' she agreed.

His blue gaze raked over her. 'You've lost weight,' he observed.

'I get sick in the mornings, but it usually wears off by mid-afternoon.'

'Yet you're expecting to carry on working?'

'I'll manage,' she said stubbornly. 'Most women do.'

'And after the birth—what then? Will your baby take second place to your career?'

'I can't say what will happen,' she said quietly. 'All I do know is that a child shouldn't have to take second place to anything.'

They stared at one another and for a moment Ellie thought he was actually going to say something *nice*, but she was wrong.

'You're going to have to update your wardrobe if you're to make a convincing bride, but that shouldn't be a problem. As the future Mrs Sarantos, you'll get unlimited access to my credit card. Does that turn you on?'

Ellie glared as she met his sardonic smile. 'Will you please stop making me sound like some kind of gold-digger?'

'Oh, come on, Ellie,' he said, and briefly some of the harshness left his voice. 'Didn't you ever learn to make the best out of a bad situation?'

She felt a twist of pain as she turned away. Didn't he realise he was talking to the queen of the positive spin? That she'd spent her life trying not to be influenced by a mother who was steeped in bitterness and regret. And hadn't she vowed that her own life would be different? That she would make something of herself? She would be strong and most of all...*independent*. And now here she was, tying herself to a cold and unfeeling man because she needed security.

But that didn't matter. None of it did. She was going to do whatever it took to give her baby a better life than the one she'd known.

Her heart clenched.

Even if it meant marrying someone who seemed to despise her.

CHAPTER SIX

ELLIE'S NEW LIFE began the minute Alek agreed to marry her and it felt like waking up in a parallel universe.

No more travelling across London, or a sticky train journey home to the New Forest. He didn't do public transport, did he? And neither would the woman who was carrying his child. A sleek limo was ordered to take her home, but not before Alek insisted she eat something. Her attempts to tell him she wasn't hungry fell on deaf ears and he sent Vasos out for warm bread, tiny purple grapes and a rich chickpea spread, which Ellie fell on with a moan of greed. She ate the lot and looked up to find him studying her.

'You're obviously not looking after yourself properly,' he said repressively. 'Forget working out your notice and move up here straight away. It makes perfect sense.'

'I can't leave Bridget in the lurch. She's been very kind to me. I'll need to give her a month's notice.'

He hadn't been happy about that, just as he hadn't been happy when she'd refused the wad of banknotes he'd tried to press on her for any *expenses*.

'Please don't try to give me money in the street, Alek,' she hissed. 'I'm not some kind of hooker. And while we're on the subject, I'm going to want my own room when I move into your apartment.' The look of surprise on his face had been almost comical. 'And that's a requirement,' she added tartly. 'Not a request.'

It was late when the car eventually dropped her off in the New Forest—too late to speak to Bridget, but Ellie's plan of telling her boss the following day was blown when Bridget walked into the shop with an expression Ellie had never seen before. The fifty-something widow who had treated her like the daughter she'd never had looked as if she was about to burst with excitement.

'Sweet saints in all heaven—why didn't you tell me?' Bridget demanded, her Irish accent still discernible, even after three decades of living in England.

'Tell you what?' questioned Ellie, her skin prickling with an instinctive dread.

'That you're going to be married! And to a handsome Greek, no less! My, but you're a secretive one, Miss Brooks.'

Ellie gripped the glass counter, forgetting the smudgy marks her fingers would leave behind. 'But how—?' She swallowed as she asked a question to which she already knew the answer. 'How did you find out?'

'How do you think?' questioned Bridget, followed by a quick demonstration of her explosive laugh. 'I got a call from the man himself late last night. He woke me out of a deep sleep, but he's so full of the Greek blarney that I told him I didn't mind a bit! He said he needs you at his side and he's offering to compensate me so that you can leave early. Why, I can get ten shop assistants for the money he's giving me—and still have plenty left over for the extension for the tea room! He's a very generous man, Ellie—and you're a very lucky woman.'

Ellie felt sick. Lucky? She felt about as lucky as someone who'd just tossed their winning lottery ticket onto a roaring fire. But she wasn't stupid. Bridget didn't care about her giving a full four weeks' notice, because Alek's offer had wiped out all other considerations. What price is friendship or loyalty in the face of all that hard cash? Was that what made him so cynical? she wondered—knowing everything had a price tag and if he paid enough, he could get exactly what he wanted?

'I've got a girl coming in from the village tomorrow,' continued Bridget chattily. 'It's all sorted.'

Ellie wondered how her boss would react if she told her the truth. *We've only had sex the once and we weren't supposed to see each other*

*again. He's only marrying me because there's a
baby on the way.*

But what good would that do? Why disillusion
someone for the sake of it? Surely it would be
best to repay Bridget's kindness by letting her
think this was what she really wanted. Oughtn't
she at least act out the fairy tale—even if she
didn't believe in it herself?

'It's very sweet of you to be so understanding,
Bridget,' she said.

'Nonsense. It's an absolute pleasure to see you
so settled and happy. Come round to the cottage
tonight and we'll have a slap-up meal, to cele-
brate.'

After work, Ellie went upstairs to her little flat
and, sure enough, there was a text message waiting on her phone.

I've sorted things out with your boss. Car arriving
for you at eleven tomorrow morning. Make sure
you're ready to leave. Alek.

If she'd thought it would make any difference,
she might have been tempted to ping back a

stinging reply, but Ellie was too tired to try. Why waste energy fighting the inevitable?

She packed up her meagre wardrobe, then went round to Bridget's hobbit-sized cottage for a vegetarian goulash. Afterwards, as she walked home in the warm summer evening, she looked up at the star-spangled sky with a feeling of wistfulness. She was going to miss the beauty of the forest—with all those cute ponies which wandered around and then stood in the middle of the road, regularly bringing all the traffic to a standstill as they swished their feathery tails. She'd always dreamed she might one day live in a big city, but never in circumstances like this. Her future lay ahead like a big uncharted map, and she felt scared.

Yet the sleep she fell into was deep and she was startled awake by the sound of a car horn beeping from beneath her open window. She staggered out of bed and hastily pulled on a robe. She had overslept and the driver was obviously here.

Except that it wasn't the driver. Ellie waited until the sickness had passed before poking her head out of the window, her breath catching in her throat when she saw Alek himself. He was leaning against a dark green sports car and it was just like the first time she'd seen him—when he'd been off duty in the spa hotel and she'd been trying very hard not to stare.

Dark shades covered his eyes and faded jeans clung to the muscular contours of his long legs. His shirtsleeves were rolled up to display powerful forearms and his hair glinted blue-black in the bright sunshine. Liquid desire began to unfold in the base of her belly—warm and unwanted and much too potent.

'Oh,' she said coolly, because she didn't want to feel this way when she looked at him. She wanted to feel *nothing*. 'It's you.'

Lifting up his shades, he narrowed his eyes against the bright light. 'I've had better greetings,' he said drily. 'Why don't you open the door and I'll come up and collect your stuff?'

'There's a key on the top ledge,' she said, withdrawing her head and grabbing some clothes as she headed for the bathroom. By the time she emerged, washed and dressed—he was standing in the middle of her sitting room, not looking in the least bit repentant.

She slammed her soap bag onto the table and turned on him, her growing temper fuelled by the arrogant look on his face. 'How dare you ring up my boss and offer her money to release me from my contract, when I told you I wanted to work out my notice?' she demanded. 'Does it give you a kick to be so *controlling*?'

'If you can give me a single valid objection,' he drawled, 'other than the mild wounding to your ego—then I'll listen. But you can't, can you, Ellie? You've been sick every morning and you look like hell, but you still want to carry on. Not the greatest advertisement for a cake shop, is it—unless you're trying to drive away the customers?' He glanced down at the two battered suitcases which were standing in the middle of the floor. 'This all you've got?'

'No, there are several Louis Vuitton trunks next door,' she said sarcastically.

He picked them up as easily as if they were full

of feathers, rather than the entire contents of her world. 'Come on. The car's waiting.'

She took the keys downstairs to the shop, where Bridget was showing the new assistant all the different cupcakes. The Strawberry Shortcake and the Lemon Lovely. The Chocolate Nemesis and the bestselling Cherry Whirl. It was farewell to a simple life and a great leap into a sophisticated unknown, and Ellie's chest felt tight with emotion as the Irishwoman hugged her, before waving her off in the shiny car.

The car roof was down and the noise of the traffic made conversation difficult but that was a relief because Ellie had no desire to talk and, besides, what would she say? How did you start a conversation with a man you barely knew in circumstances such as these? Staring out of the window, she watched as trees and fields gave way to tall buildings which shimmered in the summer sunshine like distant citadels.

Their journey took them through South Kensington, a place she'd once visited on a school trip. Thirty-five boisterous children had spent the morning in the Natural History Museum and afterwards had been allowed to descend on the museum shop. Ellie had used all her pocket money to buy her mother an expensive little bar of soap in the shape of a dinosaur. But the gift had failed to please. Apparently, it had reminded her—yet again—of all the things which were missing in her life. Ellie remembered her mother staring at the tiny bar as if it had been contaminated. Her voice had been bitter, her face contorted with a rage which was never far from the surface. *If your father had married me, you could have afforded to buy me something which was bigger than a walnut!*

And wasn't that memory reason enough to be grateful that Alek wasn't washing his hands of his responsibilities? Despite his authoritarian attitude, he was stepping up to the mark and shouldering his share of the life they had inadvertently created. He wasn't planning to never pay a penny towards his baby's upkeep, or never bother keeping in touch, was he? She stole a glance at his rugged profile. He wasn't *all* bad. And following

Leabharlanna Poibli Chathair Baile Átha Cliath

Dublin City Public Libraries

on from that wave of appreciation came another, which was rather more unwelcome, especially when his thigh tensed over the accelerator. He was so unbelievably *hot* and she hadn't really stopped to think about what the reality of that might be, when she was closeted together with him in his apartment. Could desire be switched off, like a tap? Or would close contact only increase her awareness of just how gorgeous the father of her unborn child was?

Alek lived in Knightsbridge and his apartment was everything Ellie had expected and more, although nothing could have prepared her for its sheer size and opulence. Even the relative luxury of The Hog paled into insignificance when compared to each high-ceilinged room which seemed to flow effortlessly into the next. Squashy velvet sofas stood on faded silken rugs and everywhere you looked were beautiful objects. On a small table was a box inlaid with mother-of-pearl and a small gilded egg studded with stones of emerald and blue. She blinked at it as it sparkled brightly in the sunshine. Surely those stones weren't *real*?

She wanted to ask, but it seemed rude—as if she were sizing up the place and trying to work out its worth. But it wasn't the value so much as the beauty which took her breath away. Everywhere she looked were paintings of places she'd longed to visit—upmarket versions of the posters she'd had hanging in her room at the hostel. Leafy streets in Paris and iconic churches in Rome, as well as the unbelievable architecture of Venice reflected in the dappled water of the canals.

She looked at them longingly. 'Your paintings are amazing.'

'Thank you.' He inclined his head—the tone of his voice altering slightly, as if her comment had surprised him. 'It's something of a hobby of mine. You are fond of art?'

She bit back the defensive remark which hovered on her lips. Did he think someone who worked in the service industry was incapable of appreciating art, or that you had to be wealthy to enjoy it? 'I enjoy visiting galleries when I get the chance,' she said stiffly. 'Though I've never seen stuff like this in someone's home.'

But then she'd never been in a home like this. She walked over to one of the windows which framed a stunning view of the park and when she turned round it was to find him watching her, his blue eyes giving nothing away.

'I take it you approve?'

'How could I not?' She shrugged, trying not to be affected by the intensity of that sapphire gaze. 'It's remarkable. Did you design it yourself?'

'I can't take any of the credit, I'm afraid.' His smile was bland. 'I had someone do that for me. A woman called Alannah Collins.'

Ellie nodded. Of course he did. Men like Alek didn't choose their own wallpaper or spend ages deliberating where to position the sofas. They paid for someone else to do it. Just as he paid shop owners to release their staff early from a contract. He could do what the hell he liked, couldn't he? All he had to do was to take out his chequebook. 'She's a very talented designer,' she said.

'She is.' He narrowed his eyes. 'So I take it you'll be able to tolerate living here for a while?'

'Who knows?' she answered lightly. 'We might be wanting to kill each before the week is out.'

'We might.' There was a heartbeat of a pause. 'Or we might find infinitely more satisfying ways to sublimate our...frustrations. What do you think, Ellie?'

His words were edged with mockery but there was a very real sense of sexual challenge sparking beneath that cool stare, and of course she was tempted by that look.

But even stronger than temptation was Ellie's overwhelming sense of *disorientation* as he flirted with her. Seeing him in his fancy home made it hard to believe the circumstances which had brought her here. Had he really arrived at her humble room in the staff hostel and then had sex with her on that single bed? It seemed like a muddled dream to remember him pulling urgently at her clothing, like a man out of control. She remembered the anger on his face and then the sudden transformation as his rage had given way to a passion which had left her crying in his arms afterwards.

But men could feel passion in the heat of the moment and then turn it off once their appetite had been satisfied, couldn't they? She didn't know a whole heap about sex, but she knew that much and she had to remember that she was vulnerable as far as Alek was concerned. They might have come together as equals that day, but they weren't really equals. She might soon be wearing his wedding ring but that was only a symbol. It didn't *mean* anything. It certainly didn't mean any of the things a wedding band was *supposed* to mean. She needed to keep her emotional distance. She *had* to, if she wanted to protect herself from getting hurt.

'Just to be clear.' She met the blue gleam of his eyes. 'I meant what I said about wanting my own room. So if you're thinking of trying to persuade me otherwise, I'm afraid you'll be wasting your time.'

He gave a wry smile. 'On balance, I think I agree with you. I'm beginning to think that sharing a room with you would only complicate an already complicated situation.'

Ellie felt a wave of something very feminine and contrary flaring through her as she followed him from the huge reception room. Couldn't he at least have *pretended* to be disappointed, rather than appearing almost *relieved*? With difficulty she dragged her gaze away from his powerful back and forced herself to look at all the different things he was showing her. The plush cinema with its huge screen. The black marble fittings in the shamelessly masculine kitchen. The modern dining room, which didn't look as if it was used very much—with tall silver candlesticks standing on a beautiful gleaming table. On the wall of his study, different clocks were lined up to show the time zones of all the world's major cities and his desk contained a serious amount of paperwork. He explained that there was a swimming pool in the basement of the building, as well as a fully equipped gym.

The bedroom she was allocated wasn't soft or girly—and why would it be?—but at least it was restful. The bed was big, the view spectacular. The en-suite bathroom had snowy towels and expensive bottles of bath oil and she thought about how perfect everything looked. And then there was her. Standing there in her jeans and T-shirt, she felt like a cobweb which had blown onto a line of clean washing.

'Do you like it?' he questioned.

'I can't imagine anyone not liking it. It's beautiful.' She ran her fingertip along a delicate twist of coloured glass which served no useful purpose other than to capture the light and reflect it back in rainbow rays. 'I just can't imagine how a baby is going to fit in here.'

His gaze followed the line of her fingers. 'Neither can I. But I wasn't planning on having a baby when I bought this place.'

'You didn't think that one day you might have a family of your own? I don't mean like this, obviously—'

'Obviously,' he interrupted tightly. 'And the answer is no. Not every man feels the need to lock himself into family life—particularly when so few families are happy.'

'That's a very cynical point of view, Alek.'

'You think so? Why, was your own child-hood so happy?' His gaze bore into her. 'Let me guess. A cosy English village where everyone knew each other? A cottage with roses growing around the door?'

'Hardly.' She gave a short laugh. 'I didn't meet my father until I was eighteen and when I did I wished I hadn't bothered.'

His eyes had narrowed. 'Why not?'

It was a story she wasn't proud of. Correction. It was one she was almost ashamed of. She knew it was illogical, but if you were unloved, then didn't that automatically make you unlovable? *Didn't the fault lie within her?* But she pushed that rogue thought away as she had been trying to do for most of her adult life. And there was no reason to keep secrets from Alek. She wasn't try-ing to impress him, because he'd already made it clear that he no longer wanted her. And if you moved past that rather insulting fact—didn't that mean she could be herself, instead of trying to be the person she thought she *ought* to be?

'I'd hate to shock you,' she said flippantly.

His voice was dry. 'Believe me, I am not easily shocked.'

She watched as the filmy drapes moved in a cloud-like blur at the edges of the giant windows. 'My father was a businessman—quite a successful one by all accounts—and my mother worked as his secretary, but she was also his...' She shrugged as she met his quizzical expression. 'It sounds so old-fashioned now, but she was his mistress.'

'Ah,' he said, in the tone of a man addressing a subject on which he was already an expert. 'His mistress.'

'That's right. It was the usual thing. He set her up in a flat. He bought her clothes and in particular—underwear. They used to go out for what was euphemistically known as "lunch," which I gather didn't make her very popular back at the office. Sometimes he even managed to get away for part of a weekend with her, though of course she was always on her own at Christmas and during vacations. She told me all this one night when she'd been drinking.'

'So what happened?' he questioned, diplomatically ignoring the sudden tremble in her voice. 'How come you came along?'

Caught up in a tale she hadn't thought about in a long time, Ellie sat down heavily on the bed. The Egyptian cotton felt soft as she rested her palms against it and met the cool curiosity in Alek's eyes. 'She wanted him to divorce his wife, but he wouldn't. He kept telling her that he'd have to wait for his children to leave home—again, the usual story. So she thought she'd give him a little encouragement.'

'And she got pregnant?'

'She got pregnant,' she repeated and saw the look on his face. 'And before you say anything— I did not set out to repeat history. Believe me, the last thing I wanted was to recreate my own childhood. What happened between us was—'

'An accident,' he said, almost roughly. 'Yes, I know that. Go on.'

She'd lost the thread of what she'd been saying and it took her a couple of seconds to pick it up again. 'I think she mistakenly thought that he'd get used to having a baby. That he might even be pleased…evidence of his virility…that kind of thing. But he wasn't. He already had three children he was putting through school and a wife with an expensive jewellery habit. He told her…'

Ellie's voice tailed off. She remembered that awful night of her birthday when her mother had seen off the best part of a bottle of gin and started blubbing—telling her stuff which no child should ever hear. She had buried it deep in the recesses of her own mind, but now it swam to the surface—like dark scum which had been submerged too long.

'He told her to get rid of it. Or rather…to get rid of me,' she said, her bright, pointless smile fading as her mother's words reverberated round her head. *And I should have listened to him! If I'd known what lay ahead, I damned well would have listened to him!* 'I think she thought he'd change his mind, but he didn't. He stopped paying the rent on my mother's apartment and told his wife about the affair—thus effectively curtailing any thoughts of blackmail. Then they moved to another part of the country and that was the end of that.'

'He didn't keep in contact?'

'Nope. It was different in those days, before social media really took off—it's easy to lose touch with someone. There was no maintenance—and my mother was too proud to take him to court. She said she'd already lost so much that she wouldn't give him the satisfaction of seeing her begging. She said we would manage just fine, but of course—it's never that simple.'

'But you said you saw him? When you were eighteen?'

Ellie didn't answer for a moment, because this territory was not only forbidden—it was unmarked. She wondered whether she should tell him—but how could she not? She hadn't talked about it with anyone before because she didn't want to look as if she was drowning in self-pity, but maybe Alek had a right to know.

'I did see him,' she said slowly. 'After my mother died, I tracked him down and wrote to him. Said I'd like to meet him. I was slightly surprised when he agreed.' And slightly scared, too, because she'd built him up in her head to be some kind of hero. Maybe she'd been longing for the closeness she'd never had with her mother. Perhaps she had been as guilty as the next person of wanting a fairy tale which didn't exist. The big reunion which was going to make everything in her life better.

'What happened?'

She narrowed her eyes. 'You really want to know?'

'I do. You tell a good story,' he said, surprisingly.

She wanted to tell him that it wasn't a *story*, but when she stopped to think about it—maybe it was. Life was a never-ending story—wasn't that how the old cliché went? She cleared her throat. 'There was no psychic connection between us. No sense that here was the person whose genes I shared. We didn't even look alike. He sat on the other side of a noisy table in a café at Waterloo station and told me that my mother was a conniving bitch who had almost ruined his life.'

'And that was it?' he asked after a long moment.

'Pretty much. I tried asking about my half-sister and half-brothers and anyone would have thought I'd asked him for the PIN number for his savings account, from the way he reacted.' He had stood up then with an ugly look on his face, but the look had been tinged with satisfaction— as if he'd been *glad* of an excuse to be angry with her. She remembered him knocking against the table and her untouched cappuccino slopping everywhere in a frothy puddle. 'He told me never to contact him again. And then he left.'

Alek heard the determinedly nonchalant note in her voice and something twisted darkly in his gut. Was it recognition? A realisation that everyone carried their own kind of pain, but that most of it was hidden away? Suddenly her fierce ambition became understandable—an ambition which had been forced into second place by the baby. He felt a pang of guilt as he recalled how cavalier he'd been about her losing her job. Suddenly, he could understand her insistence on marriage— a request which must have been fuelled by the uncertainty of her own formative years. Not because she wanted the cachet of being his wife, but because she wanted to give her own baby the security she'd never had.

But recognising something didn't change anything. He needed to be clear about the facts and so did she—and the most important fact she needed to realise was that he could never do the normal stuff that women seemed to want. He might be capable of honouring his responsibility to her and the baby—but, emotionally, wasn't he cut from exactly the same cloth as her father? Hadn't he walked away from women in the past—blind to their tears and their needs?

Ellie Brooks wasn't his type, but even if she were he was the last man she needed. She needed his name on a birth certificate and she needed his money, and he could manage that. *Neh.* A bitter smile curved his lips. He could manage that very well. But if she wanted someone to provide the love and support her father had never given her, then he was the wrong person.

She had pushed the heavy fringe away from

her eyebrows. Her face was pale, he thought. And now that she no longer had those generous curves, there was a kind of fragility about her which gave her skin a curious luminosity. And suddenly, all his certainties seemed to fade away. He forgot that it was infinitely more sensible to keep his distance from her as he was overcome by a powerful desire to take her in his arms and offer her comfort.

He swallowed, his feelings confusing him. And angering him. He didn't *want* to be in thrall to anyone, but certainly not to her. Because he recognised that Ellie possessed something which no woman before her had ever possessed. *A part of him.* And didn't that give her a special kind of power? A power she could so easily abuse if he wasn't careful.

He walked quickly towards the door, realising that he needed to get the hell out of there. 'You'd better unpack,' he said abruptly. 'And then we need to sit down and discuss the practicalities of you living here.'

CHAPTER SEVEN

WITH A SPEED which left her slightly dazed, Alek took over Ellie's life. He organised a doctor and a credit card. He filled in all the requisite forms required for their upcoming wedding and booked the register office. But it quickly dawned on Ellie that the most important *practicality* of living with the Greek tycoon was an ability to be happy with her own company.

'I work long hours,' he told her. 'And I travel. A lot. You'll need to be able to amuse yourself and not come running to me because you're bored. Understand?'

Biting back her indignation at being spoken to as if she were some kind of mindless puppet, Ellie told herself that snapping at him was only going to make a difficult situation worse. Bad enough that he prowled around the place looking like a sex god, without taking him to task over his patronising comments. She was trying very hard to give him the benefit of the doubt—telling herself that perhaps he didn't mean to be quite so insulting. That he was a powerful man who was clearly used to issuing orders which he expected to be obeyed. And at first, she did exactly that.

During those early days in his Knightsbridge penthouse, she was still too disorientated by the speed at which her life had changed to object to his steamrollering approach to life. She was introduced as his fiancée to the confusingly large number of staff who worked for him both in and outside his organisation and she tried to remember everyone's name.

There were cleaners who moved noiselessly around the vast apartment—like ghosts carrying buckets—and a woman whose job was to keep his fridge and wine cellar stocked. There was the doctor who insisted on visiting her at home—unheard of!—and told her she should take it easy, and these instructions she followed to the letter. She made the most of her free time. She realised it was the first time she'd ever had a prolonged break—or enjoyed a guilt-free session of relaxation—and she concentrated on settling into her new habitat like a cuckoo finding its way round a new and very luxurious nest.

But the baby still felt as if it weren't happening, even though she was now in possession of a glossy black and white photo showing what looked like a cashew nut, attached to the edge of a dark lake. And when she looked into the icy beauty of Alek's eyes, it was hard to believe that the tiny life growing inside her was somehow connected with him. Would he love his baby? she found herself wondering. Was he even *capable* of love?

He's capable of sex, prompted a whispering voice inside her head—but determinedly she blocked out the thought. She wasn't going to think of him that way. She just wasn't.

The friendly concierge in the lobby gave her a street map and she started exploring Kensington and Chelsea, as well as the nearby park, where the leaves on the trees were showing the first hints of gold. She began visiting the capital's galleries with enough time on her hands to really make the most of them, which she'd never had before.

Each morning, Alek left early for the office and would return late, a pair of dark-rimmed reading glasses giving him a surprisingly sexy, geeky look as he carried in the sheaf of papers he'd been studying in the car. He would disappear into his room to shower and change and then—surprisingly—disappear into the kitchen to cook them both dinner. An extensive repertoire of dishes began to appear each evening—one involving aubergine and cheese, which quickly became Ellie's favourite. He told her that he'd learnt to cook at sixteen, when he'd been working in a restaurant and the chef had told him that a man who could feed himself was a man who would survive.

His skill in the kitchen wasn't what she had been expecting and it took some getting used to—sitting and politely discussing the day's happenings over dinner, like two people on a first date who were on their best behaviour. It was like being in some kind of dream. As if it were all happening to someone else.

It was just unfortunate that Ellie's body didn't feel a bit dreamlike, but uncomfortably real. Her reservations about living with him had been realised and she was achingly aware of him. How could she not be? His presence was impossible to ignore. Much as she tried to deny it, he was her every fantasy come to life. Worse still, she'd had a brief taste of what lovemaking could be like in Alek's arms, and it had left her hungry and wanting more. And daily exposure to him was only reinforcing that hunger.

She saw him first thing when he was newly showered and dressed, with his dark hair slicked back and his skin smelling of lemon. She saw him sitting at the breakfast bar, sliding heavy gold cufflinks through one of his pristine shirts—and her heart would give a powerful contraction of blatant longing. Did he know that? Did he realise that inside she was berating herself for having insisted on a stupid no-sex rule? Had she imagined a hint of amusement dancing in the depths of those sapphire eyes when he looked at her? As if he was enjoying some private joke at her expense—silently taunting her with the knowledge that he could cope with sensual deprivation far better than her.

It was weekends which were hardest, when his failure to leave for the office left a gaping hole in the day ahead, along with the distraction of having him around without a break. This was when breakfast became a more awkward meal than usual. Was she imagining him staring at her intently, or was that just wishful thinking on her part? Had he deliberately left a button of his silk shirt unbuttoned, so that a smooth golden triangle of skin was revealed? Ellie would feel her breasts tingling with a hateful kind of hunger as he slid a jar of marmalade across the table towards her. She remembered what he'd said about faking affection for the wedding photos. No. She definitely wasn't going to have a problem with that.

On the third weekend, she was as edgy as an exam candidate and glad to get out of the apartment for Alek's suggested trip to the Victoria and Albert. It was a museum she'd longed to visit again, even though this time the statues were wasted on her. She kept looking at the carved and stony features of various kings and dignitaries and comparing them unfavourably with the beautiful features of the man by her side. Afterwards, they walked to an open-air restaurant for a late lunch and she had to fight to quash her stupid desire to have him touch her again. She thought about their wedding and their wedding night, and wondered how she was going to cope with *that.*

This time next month I'll be his wife, she thought. *Even though both of us seem determined not to talk about it.*

The sun was dipping lower in the sky as they walked back across the park, but when she got back to the apartment she found herself unable to get comfortable. Her feet were aching and she was wriggling around restlessly on the sofa.

She didn't know what she was expecting when Alek walked across the room and sat down next to her, lifting her bare feet into his lap and beginning to massage each one in turn. It was the first time he'd touched her in a long time and, despite her thoughts of earlier, her instinctive reaction was to freeze, even though her heart had started hammering. Could he hear its wild beat or maybe even see it, beneath her thin T-shirt? Was that why he gave that slow half-smile?

But her initial tension dissolved the instant the warm pad of his thumb started caressing her insole and once she realised that this wasn't a seduction but simply a foot massage, she just lay back and enjoyed it. It felt like bliss and she found herself thinking how ironic it was that all his money couldn't buy something as good as this. Did he realise how much she loved the thoughtful gesture, even though she'd done her best to conceal her squirming pleasure from him? Was he aware that small kindnesses like these were the dangerous blocks which made her start building impossible dreams?

The following Monday, she was drinking ginger tea at the kitchen table when he glanced up from his newspaper and narrowed his eyes.

'About these new clothes you're supposed to be buying,' he said.

'Maternity clothes?'

'Not quite yet. I meant pretty clothes,' he said. 'Isn't that what we agreed? Something to make you look the part of a Sarantos bride. Not long to go now.'

'I know that.'

'You haven't shown very much interest in your wedding so far.'

'It's difficult to get enthusiastic about a ceremony which feels fake.'

He didn't rise to the taunt. 'I thought you'd be itching to get your hands on my chequebook.'

'Sorry to disappoint you,' she said in a hollow voice, thinking about the foot massage. Didn't he realise that something that simple and intimate was worth far more to her than his money? Of course he didn't. It suited him much more to imagine her salivating over his credit card.

He put his newspaper down. 'Well, there's no point in putting it off any longer. I can arrange for Alannah to take you shopping and you can

choose your wedding dress at the same time, if
you like. You'll find she has a superb eye.'

'You mean I don't?'

He frowned. 'That wasn't what I said.'

'But that's what you implied, isn't it? Poor little
Ellie—snatched up from rural Hampshire with
no idea how to shop for clothes which might
make her believable as the wife of the powerful
Greek!' She stood up quickly—too quickly—and
had to steady herself. 'Well, I'm perfectly capable
of buying my own clothes—and my own wedding dress. So why don't you give me your precious credit card and I'll see if I can do it justice?
I'll go out this morning and just spend, spend,
spend like the stereotypical gold-digger you're
so fond of portraying!'

'Ellie—'

She stalked off into her room and slammed
the door very noisily, but when she came out
again sometime later it was to find him still sitting there—the pile of newspapers almost completely read.

'I thought you were going into the office this morning,' she said.

'Not any more,' he said. 'I'm taking you shopping.'

'I don't want you to…' Her voice faltered, because when his blue eyes softened like that, he was making her feel stuff she didn't want to feel.

'Don't want me to what?'

She didn't want him standing on the other side of a curtain while she tried to cram her awkward-looking body into suitable clothes. She didn't want to see the disbelieving faces of the sales assistants as they wondered what someone like him was doing with someone like her. Shopping for clothes was a nightmare experience at the best of times, but throwing the arrogant Alek into the mix would make it a million times worse. 'Hang around outside the changing room,' she said.

'Why not?'

She shrugged. Why not tell him the truth? 'I'm self-conscious about my body.'

He poured himself a cup of coffee. 'Why?'

'Because I *am*, that's why.' She glared at him.

'Most women are—especially when they're pregnant.'

His gaze slid over her navel, his expression suggesting he wasn't used to looking at a woman in a way which wasn't sexual. 'I should have thought that my own reaction to your body would have been enough to reassure you that I find it very attractive indeed.'

'That isn't the point,' she said, unwilling to point out that lately he hadn't shown the slightest interest in her body, because wouldn't that make her seem *vulnerable*? 'I'm not willing to do a Cinderella transformation scene with you as an audience.'

He opened his mouth and then, shutting it again, he sighed. 'Okay. So what if I act as your chauffeur for the day? I'll drive you to a department store and park up somewhere and wait. And you can text me when you're done. How does that sound?'

It sounded so reasonable that Ellie couldn't come up with a single objection and soon she was seated beside him in the car as he negotiated the morning traffic. She was slightly terrified when he dropped her off outside the store, but she'd read enough magazines to know that she was perfectly entitled to request the services of a personal shopper. And it didn't seem to matter that she was wearing jeans and a T-shirt or that her untrimmed fringe was flopping into her eyes like a sheepdog—because the elegant woman assigned to her made no judgements. She delicately enquired what Ellie's upper price limit was. And although Ellie's instinct was to go for the cheapest option, she knew Alek wouldn't thank her for shopping on a budget. He'd once drawlingly told her that it was the dream of every woman to get her hands on his credit card, so why disappoint him? Why not try to become the woman that he and his fancy friends would obviously expect her to be?

She quickly discovered how easy shopping was when you had money. You could buy the best. You could complement your outfits with soft leather shoes and pick up a delicate twist of a silk scarf which echoed the detail in a fabric.

And expensive clothes really could transform, she decided. The luscious fabrics seemed to flatter her shape, rather than highlight her defects.

The shopper persuaded her into the dresses she usually rejected on the grounds that jeans were more practical, and Ellie found she liked the swish of the delicate fabrics brushing against her skin. She bought all the basic clothes she needed and then picked out a silvery-white wedding gown which did amazing things for her eyes as well as her figure. On impulse, the personal shopper draped a scarlet pashmina around her shoulders—a stole so fine it was almost transparent, and it was that addition which brought glowing life to her skin. Ellie stared at herself in the long mirror.

'It's perfect,' she said slowly.

By the time she emerged from the store wearing some of her purchases, she felt like a new woman.

She saw Alek's face change as she approached the car, accompanied by two doormen who were weighed down with armfuls of packages. His arm brushed over her back with proprietary courtesy as he held open the car door for her and she stiffened, because just that brief touch felt as if he'd branded her with the heat of his flesh. Was that why he stiffened, too? Why his eyes narrowed and a nerve began to work at his temple? She thought he might be about to touch her again—and wasn't she longing for him to do just that?—but some car had begun sounding its horn and the noise seemed to snap him out of his uncharacteristic hesitation.

He didn't say much as they drove to Bond Street, not until they were standing in front of a jeweller's window which was ablaze with the glitter of a thousand gems. And suddenly he turned to her and his face had that expression she'd seen once before, when all the cool arrogance which defined him had been replaced by a raw and naked hunger.

His finger wasn't quite steady as it drifted a slow path down over her cheek and he must have felt her shiver in response, because his eyes narrowed.

'You look…different,' he said.

'I thought that was the whole point of the exercise?' she said, more archly than she had intended. 'I have to look *credible*, don't I, as the future Mrs Sarantos?'

'But you don't, Ellie—that's the thing.' He gave her an odd kind of smile. 'You don't look credible at all. Not with that uptight expression on your face. It's not the look one might expect from a woman who is just about to marry one of the world's most eligible bachelors. There's no real joy or pleasure there, and I think we might have to remedy that. Shall we make a statement to the world about our relationship, *poulaki mou*? To show them we really do mean business?'

And before Ellie realised what was happening, he was kissing her. Kissing her in full view of the traffic and the security guard and all the upmarket shoppers who were passing them on the pavement. He had wrapped his arms tightly around her and was making her feel as if he *owned her.* The man who was so famously private was making a very public declaration. And even though her heart was pounding with joy, suddenly she felt like a possession. A woman he was putting his stamp on. *His* woman; *his* property.

She tried keeping her lips clamped shut to prevent his tongue from entering her mouth—to let him know that she was *not* a possession. That he couldn't just pick her up and put her down when he felt like it. But there was only so much resistance she could put up when he was this determined. When he was splaying his fingers over the bare skin of her back and making it tingle. His hard body was so close that a cigarette paper couldn't have come between them, and, beneath her delicate new bra, her breasts were growing heavy.

His lips were still brushing against hers and her eyelids fluttered to a close. She thought how crazy it was that so many emotions could be stimulated by a single kiss. Did he realise that she found being in his arms satisfying in all kinds of ways? Ways which were about so much more than sex? She felt safe and secure. Like nothing could ever hurt her while Alek was around.

And it was his strength rather than his sensuality which finally melted the last of her reservations. She kissed him back with fervour and passion and, in the process, completely forgot where she was. Her hands reached up to frame his head and she moaned softly as she circled her hips against him, so that in the end it was Alek who pulled back—his eyes smouldering with blue fire.

'Oh, my,' he said softly, and a distinctive twang of North Atlantic entered his gravelly Greek accent. 'Maybe I should have kissed you back at the apartment, if I'd known that this was the reaction I was going to get.'

His words broke the spell and Ellie jerked away with a bitter feeling of self-recrimination. She had allowed herself to be seduced again when this was nothing but a game to him. A stupid, meaningless game. He had kissed her to make a point and she wasn't sure if it had been a demonstration of power, or just payback time for her expensive new wardrobe. But either way, she was going to get hurt if she wasn't careful. Badly hurt.

She rose up on tiptoe in her new leather pumps, placing her lips to his ear.

'What was that all about?' she hissed.

'Want me to draw a diagram for you?' he murmured back.

'That won't be necessary.' She moved her mouth closer to his ear, tempted to take a nip at its perfect lobe. 'Sex just *complicates* matters. That was the deal—remember?'

'I think I might be prepared to overlook the deal in view of the response I just got.'

'Well, I wouldn't—and there's something you'd better understand, Alek.' She swallowed, trying to inject conviction into her voice. 'Which is that I wouldn't go to bed with you if you were the last man standing.'

He tipped his head back so that she was caught in the crossfire of his eyes, the darkened blue hue backlit by the definite glitter of amusement. He lifted his fingertip to her mouth and traced it thoughtfully along the line of her lips. 'I don't think that's entirely true, do you, Ellie?'

'Yes,' she said fiercely, resisting the urge to

bite his finger, afraid that if she did she might just start sucking it. 'It's true.'

He took her hand in his and she wanted to snatch it away like a sulky child. But the door-man was still watching them and she knew that if she was to play the part of fiancée convinc-ingly, then she had no choice other than to let him carry on stroking her fingers like that and pretend it wasn't turning her on.

'Let's go and buy your wedding ring,' he said.

CHAPTER EIGHT

THE RING WAS a glittering band of diamonds and the silvery shoes which matched her wedding dress had racy scarlet soles. Ellie touched her fingertips to her professionally styled hair, which had been snipped and blow-dried. She looked like a bride, all right, but a magazine version of a bride—untraditional and slightly edgy. The silver dress and scarlet pashmina gave her a sophisticated patina she wasn't used to and projected an image which wasn't really *her*. But the unfamiliar sleekness of her appearance did nothing to subdue the butterflies which were swarming in her stomach. They'd been building in numbers ever since she and Alek had said their vows earlier, with Vasos and another Sarantos employee standing as their only witnesses.

Strange to believe they were now man and

wife—and that fifty of Alek's closest friends were assembling at the upmarket restaurant they'd chosen to stage their wedding party. And if it felt like a sham, that's because it was.

And yet...

Yet...

She stared down at her sparkling wedding band. When he'd kissed her so passionately in Bond Street—hadn't that felt like something? Even though she'd tried telling herself that he'd only done it to make a point, that hadn't been enough to dull her reaction to him. She had nearly gone up in flames as sexual hunger had overpowered her and a wave of emotion had crashed over her with such force that she'd felt positively weak afterwards. It was as if the rest of the world hadn't existed in those few minutes afterwards, and wasn't that...*dangerous*?

The peremptory knock on her bedroom door broke into her thoughts and she opened it to find Alek standing there—broodingly handsome in his beautifully cut wedding suit, with a tie the colour of storm clouds.

'Ready?' he questioned.

She told herself she wasn't waiting for him to comment on her appearance—but what else would account for the sudden plummeting of her heart? She'd blamed pre-wedding jitters for his failure to compliment her the first time he'd seen her in her wedding dress. But now that they were man and wife, surely he could have said *something*. Had she secretly been longing for his eyes to light up and him to tell her that she made a halfway passable bride? Or was she hoping he'd make another pass at her, only this time she might not get so angry with him? She might just let him carry on...and they could consummate their marriage and satisfy the law, as well as their hungry bodies.

She swallowed. Yes. If the truth be known, she had wanted exactly that. From the time they'd returned from that shopping trip right up to the brief civil ceremony this morning, she'd been like a cat on a hot tin roof. She'd been convinced he would try to renegotiate the separate bedrooms rule, but she had been wrong. Despite her feisty words, he must have known from the way she'd responded to his kiss that she'd changed her mind. That all he needed to do was to kiss her one more time and she would be his. But Alek wasn't a man whose behaviour you could predict. It felt as if he had been deliberately keeping his distance from her ever since. Skirting around her as if she were some unexploded device he didn't dare approach. Even when he'd put the ring on her finger this morning in front of the registrar, she had received nothing more than a cool and perfunctory kiss on each cheek.

She gave him her best waitress smile. 'Yes, I'm ready.'

'Then let's go.'

She felt sick with nerves at the thought of meeting all his friends, especially since the only person she'd invited was Bridget, who wasn't able to attend because the new assistant still wasn't confident enough to be left on her own. Ellie picked up her handbag. She'd thought about inviting some of her New Forest friends, but how to go about explaining why she was marrying a man who was little more than a stranger to her? Wouldn't one of her girlfriends quickly suss that it was odd not to be giggling and cuddling up to a man you were planning to spend the rest of your life with? No. She didn't want pity or a well-meaning mate trying to talk her out of what was the only sensible solution to her predicament. She was going to have to go it alone. To be at her sparkling best and not let any of her insecurities show. She was going to have to make the marriage look as real as possible to *his* friends—and surely that wasn't beyond her capabilities to play a convincing part in front of people who didn't know her?

'Remind me again who's going,' she said as their car began to slip through the early evening traffic.

'Niccolò and Alannah—property tycoon and interior designer,' he said. 'Luis and Carly—he's the ex world champion racing driver and she's his medic wife. Oh, and Murat.'

Ellie forced a smile. Didn't he know any *normal* people? 'The Sultan?'

'That's right. And because of that, security will be tight.'

'You mean, I'll be frisked going into my own wedding party?'

He'd been staring out of the window and drumming his fingertips over one taut thigh and Ellie wished he'd say something equally flippant—anything to dispel this weird *atmosphere* between them. But when he spoke it was merely to resume a clipped tally of the guest list. 'There are people flying in from Paris, New York, Rome, Sicily—'

'And Greece, of course?' she prompted.

He shook his head. 'No. Not Greece.'

'But...that's where you come from.'

'So what? I left there a long time ago, and rarely visit these days.'

'But—'

'Look, can we just dispense with the interrogation, Ellie?' he interrupted coolly. 'I'm not really inclined to answer any more questions and, anyway, we're here.'

'Of course,' she said, quickly turning her head to look out of the window.

Alek felt a pang of guilt as he saw her silvery shoulders tense up. Okay, maybe he *had* been short with her but she needed to realise that being questioned like that wasn't his idea of fun. His mouth flattened. But what had he expected? Wasn't this what happened when you spent prolonged time with a woman? They felt it gave them the right to chip away at things. To quiz you about stuff you didn't want to talk about, even when you made it clear that a subject was deliberately off limits.

He'd never lived with anyone before Ellie. He'd never given a home to a second toothbrush, nor had to clear out space in his closet. Even though they had their own rooms, sometimes it felt as if it were impossible to get away from her. And the stupid thing was that he didn't want to get away from her. He wanted to get closer, even though instinct was telling him that was a bad idea. She was a constant temptation. She made him want her all the time, even though she didn't flirt with him. And wasn't even *that* a turn on? She was there in the morning before he left for work, all bright-eyed and smiling as she sat drinking her ginger tea. Just as she was there at night when he got home, offering to pour him a drink, telling him that she'd started experimenting with cooking and would he like to try some? She'd asked him for tips on how to cook the aubergine dish and he had found himself leaning dangerously close to her while she stirred something in a pot, tempted to kiss the bare neck which was a few tempting inches away from him. Slowly and very subtly her presence was driving him mad. Mostly, it was driving him mad because he wanted her—and he had no one to blame but himself.

That hot-headed kiss outside the jewellers had been intended as nothing more than a distraction. If he was being honest, it had also been intended as an arrogant demonstration of his sexual mastery. To show her that he was boss and always would be. But somehow it had backfired on him. It had reactivated his desire and now he was stuck with a raging sexual hunger which kept him awake most nights, staring at the ceiling and imagining all the different things he wanted to do to her.

He knew there was nothing stopping him from acting on it. From stealing into her room when darkness had fallen. From pulling back a crisp sheet and finding her, what…naked? Or wearing some slinky little nightgown she might have bought at the same time as the killer heels and new clothes. Those occasional longing looks and accidental touches had reinforced what he'd already known…that she wanted him as much as he wanted her. Physically, at least. He was confident enough to know he could be inside her in minutes if he put his mind to it, tangling his fingers in the soft spill of her pale hair and staring down at her beautiful pale curves.

And then what?

He felt another unwanted and unfamiliar stab of his conscience, which was enough to kill his desire stone-dead. Make her fall in love with him? Break her heart as he had broken so many in the past and leave her bitter and upset? Some good that would do when Ellie, above all others, was someone he needed to keep onside. She was carrying his baby and he needed her as a friend, not as a lover.

Because something inside him had changed. He'd imagined he would feel nothing about the new life growing inside her and that he would feel disconnected from her pregnancy. But he had been wrong. Hadn't his heart clenched savagely in his chest the first time he'd seen her fingertips drift almost reflectively over her still-flat belly?

With a fascination which seemed beyond his control, he had found himself watching her when she wasn't looking. When she was curled up in an armchair reading a book and making his life seem almost...*normal*. He'd never had normal before. And hadn't he been filled with an unbearable sense of longing for the family life which had been nothing but a dark void during his own childhood? Hadn't he started wondering again whether he could give this child what he'd never had himself? And one thing was for sure: he could not break the heart of his child's mother...

The car stopped outside the restaurant and as she draped the scarlet shawl around her shoulders he found he couldn't look away. He wanted to pull her into his arms and kiss all that shiny lipstick away from her beautiful lips, but why start the evening on a false promise?

'You look...great,' he said neutrally as the driver opened the limousine door for her.

'Thanks.'

Ellie's fingers tightened around the gilt chain of her handbag. First he'd shot her down in flames and then he'd told her she looked *great*? Was that the best he could do? Why, she'd had more praise from her science teacher at school—and she was hopeless at science. Cautiously, she stepped onto the pavement, balancing carefully on her high heels, thinking how unlike the Ellie of old she must look with enough diamonds glittering on her finger to have bought her an apartment outright.

She was grateful for the armour of her expensive new clothes in a room where every other woman looked amazing—but it wasn't that which made her feel suddenly wistful. All the wives and girlfriends looked so *happy*. Did she? Did she look how a new bride was supposed to look—all dewy-eyed and serene? She wondered if anyone guessed that inside she felt as if she were clinging onto this strange new reality by the tips of her fingers.

But sometimes you built things up in your head and they weren't nearly as bad as you'd feared. The woman who'd designed Alek's apartment— Alannah—turned out to be a lot less scary than Ellie had imagined. Maybe because she was married to Niccolò da Conti, a stunningly handsome man who seemed to command almost as much attention as Alek and who clearly adored his wife.

Some of the guests were more memorable than others. Ellie stood for ages talking to Luis and Carly and discovered they were all friends going back years. When the sultan arrived—last—Ellie was overcome with nerves because she'd never met a royal before and might not have bought such high heels if she'd thought about having to curtsey in them. But Murat was charming and quickly put her at her ease, and his Welsh wife was lovely.

Ellie watched the exalted group of men joshing and laughing with one another and as she listened to their wives eagerly discussing their social calendars she tried not to feel like the outsider in their midst.

'Let me see your ring, Ellie,' said Alannah, catching hold of Ellie's hand and peering down at the glittering band. 'Gosh, it's beautiful. Those diamonds look almost blue—they're so bright.' She raised her eyes and smiled. 'So tell us about Alek's proposal—was it romantic?'

Ellie wished she'd anticipated this perfectly understandable question so that she could have prepped an answer. She didn't know how honest to be. She didn't know how much he'd already told them. She knew that apart from the faint swell of her breasts, there was no outward sign of her pregnancy. Maybe some of the women had already guessed the reason why the world's most reluctant groom had put a ring on her finger, but for some reason she didn't want to tell them. Not right now. Couldn't tonight be her fantasy? Couldn't she play the part of the shiny-eyed new bride and pretend, just this once?

So she curved a smile—and found it was stupidly easy to let her voice tremble with excitement as she allowed herself to be caught up in the memory. 'He kissed me in Bond Street and almost stopped the traffic.'

'*Really?*' Alannah smiled. 'Not *another* "get a room" moment from the famously private Alek Sarantos? Didn't I read something about him kissing you while you were working as a waitress?'

A sudden lump in her throat was making words difficult and Ellie just nodded. She wondered if Alek ever thought about that moment of passion beneath the starry sky. That split second of thoughtlessness, setting off the domino effect which had brought them to this moment. Did he regret it?

Yet as she glanced over to see him deep in conversation with Murat, she found that she *couldn't* regret what had happened, because sometimes your feelings defied logic. Something incredible had happened when she'd lain with him and she couldn't seem to scrub that memory away. He could be arrogant and cold, but there was something about him which drew her to him like a magnet, no matter how hard she tried to resist. It might be senseless to care about him, but did that mean it was wrong? Could you stop yourself from falling in love with someone, even if you knew it was a mistake?

She saw him smile at something Murat said and he responded by gesturing expansively with his hands in a way an Englishman would never do. She'd never been to Greece, but in that moment he seemed to sum up everything about that sun-washed land with its ancient history and its passions.

Yet that side of his life remained a mystery to her. He'd clammed up when she'd mentioned his birthplace on the way here. He had snapped and changed the subject and done that not very subtle thing of letting her know who had all the power in this relationship. How much did she really know about the father of her baby? She stared down at the slice of lime which was bobbing around in her tonic water. Probably as much as she knew about her own father.

But she pushed the troublesome thoughts away and tried to enter into the spirit of the evening. She nibbled on a few canapés and stood beside Alek as he made a short speech about love and marriage, with just the right touch of lightness and solemnity.

And that was the bit she found hardest. The moment when she wanted to shake off the hand which was resting lightly on her shoulders, because it was kick-starting all kinds of reactions. It was making her want to feel that extraordinary *connection* with him again. To lie with him and feel him deep inside her. To wonder why the hell she'd insisted on separate rooms—not realising that denial would only feed the hunger she felt for him.

She spoke to all the guests with just the right

amount of interest and pretended she was Ellie the trainee hotel manager again—chatting away with smiling attention. People were never terrifying if you got them on a one-to-one basis, no matter how initially intimidating they were. She met a judge, a Hollywood actress and a Spaniard named Vicente de Castilla, whose buccaneering appearance was attracting plenty of covert glances. But gorgeous as Vicente was, there was only one man who commanded Ellie's attention and she knew exactly where he was at any given point in the evening. He seemed to command all her attention and it was difficult not to stare. Beneath the fractured rainbow light of the chandeliers, his hair gleamed like jet. At one point he slowly turned his head to look at her, his blue eyes blazing as they held her in their spotlight. And she turned away, feeling curiously *exposed*...stiffening slightly when he came to stand beside her, sliding his arm around her waist with easy possession. As if he touched her like that all the time, when they both knew he didn't touch her at all.

She knew it was done to add authenticity to their marriage. She *knew* his touch meant nothing, but unfortunately her body didn't. It was sending frantic messages to her brain. It was making her want more. It was making her wish it were all real. That he'd married her because he loved her and not because there was a baby on the way.

Quickly excusing herself, she made her way to the restroom where Alannah was standing in front of the mirror, brushing her long black hair.

'Enjoying your wedding party?' she questioned.

Ellie pulled out a convincing smile as she met the other woman's denim-blue eyes. 'It's wonderful. Such a gorgeous place. And all Alek's friends seem lovely and very welcoming,' she added.

Alannah laughed. 'You don't *have* to say that—but thanks very much all the same. We're just all very happy for him, that's all. Nobody thought he would ever settle down. I expect you know that he's never really committed to anyone before? Mind you, Niccolò was exactly the same. They just need to find the right woman,' she said, pulling open the door and wiggling her fingers in a little wave of farewell.

Ellie watched the door swing closed again.

The right woman.

If only they knew. Would they all be choking into their champagne if they realised that the newlyweds were about as far apart as two people could be?

But *she* had been the one who insisted on having separate rooms, hadn't she? She'd been the one who had thought that keeping distance between them would help protect her against emotional pain. And it didn't. Because she found herself wanting Alek no matter how hard she tried not to want him.

She gazed at her reflection, thinking that her appearance betrayed nothing of her turmoil. The silvery silk dress gleamed and her professionally blow-dried hair fell in a soft cascade over her shoulders. She didn't look like herself, and she didn't feel like herself either. All she could feel was a longing so powerful that it felt like a physical pain. It might be crazy but she wasn't going to lie…and the truth was that she wanted Alek.

She closed her eyes.

She wanted more than that single encounter which had resulted in this pregnancy. She wanted something slow and precious because everything else had happened so *fast*. She'd become pregnant after that one time. She had demanded marriage and moved in with him. She'd attended doctor's appointments, taken care of herself and tried to keep busy. But she wasn't a cardboard cut-out. She still had feelings—feelings she'd tried to put on ice, only somewhere along the way they had started to melt.

So what was she going to do about it? Was she brave enough to go after what she really wanted and to hell with the consequences? Did she dare risk pain for another moment of passion?

Picking up her handbag, she walked out into the corridor where Alek's shadow fell over her and instantly she froze.

'Oh,' she said, attempting a smile. 'You startled me.'

Alek felt a pulse hammering away at his temple as he stared at her. She was close enough to touch and it was distracting. *Theos*, but it was distracting. Her hair was tumbling down over her shoulders and she had that slightly untouchable beauty of all brides. But all he could think about was the creaminess of her skin and the scent of something which smelt like roses, or cinnamon. Maybe both. He felt his throat thicken. 'I was looking for you.'

'Well…here I am,' she said, and as she met his eyes her lips parted. 'What exactly do you want?'

Alek went very still. He saw the darkening of her eyes and heard the dip of her voice, but it was more than that which told him what was on her mind. He'd been around enough women to realise when they were sending out messages of sexual availability—it was just that he hadn't been expecting it with Ellie. Not tonight. He knew that she considered the wedding a farce. That they hadn't been honest with anyone, least of all themselves. Nobody knew the real reason for this wedding, but he'd justified not telling his friends about the baby by remembering what the doctor had said—that there was a slightly higher risk of miscarriage until after the twelve-week mark. And something about those cautionary words had made him realise how much he wanted this baby—for reasons he didn't care to fathom. He realised that the life she carried inside her *mattered*. Should he tell her that? Should he?

But suddenly he wasn't thinking about the baby and neither, it seemed, was she. He could almost *see* the invitation glinting from her eyes and although he wanted her more badly than he'd ever wanted anyone—one last stab of conscience told him to hang fire. That the most sensible option would be if they ended the night as they'd begun it. Separately.

But sometimes the right decision was the wrong decision when it went against everything your body was crying out for. The ache in his groin was unbearable as he reached for her hand, which was trembling, just like his.

He studied the sheen of her fingernails before lifting his head in a clashing of eyes. 'I want you,' he said unsteadily. 'Do you have any idea how much?'

'I think I'm getting the general idea.'

'But I'm not going to do this if it's not what *you* want.' He stared at her intently. 'Do you understand?'

'Alek.' One of the silvery straps of her dress slipped off one shoulder and she pushed it back again with fingers which were trembling and her grey eyes looked wary. As if she was suddenly out of her depth. As if the words she was about to say were difficult. 'You...you're an experienced man. You must know how much I want you.'

He shook his head. 'I know that your body wants me and that physically we're very compatible. But if you're going to wake up in the morning with tears all over my pillow because you're regretting what happened, then I'll back off right now and we'll act like this conversation never happened.'

There was silence. A silence which seemed to go on for countless minutes.

'I don't want you to back off,' she whispered at last.

His heart pounded and his body grew hard. He raised her hand to his lips and although the now faint voice of his conscience made one last, weak appeal, ruthlessly he brushed it aside. 'Then let's get home,' he said roughly. 'So I can take you to bed.'

CHAPTER NINE

ALEK FELT AS if he wanted to explode but he knew he had to take it slowly.

He and Ellie had left the party almost immediately—smiling through the rose petals and rice showering down on their heads. But the journey home had been tense and silent, in direct contrast to their teasing banter at the wedding reception. He hadn't trusted himself to touch her and maybe Ellie had felt the same because she'd sat apart from him, her shoulders stiff. The tension in the car had grown and grown until it had felt as if he was having difficulty breathing. *And wasn't he terrified that she'd changed her mind?*

Her face had been paler than usual as they'd ridden up in the elevator. The space had seemed to close in on them until the ping announcing their arrival at the penthouse had broken into the silence like the chime of a mighty bell. He'd convinced himself that she *had* changed her mind as he'd unlocked the door to his apartment. But it seemed she hadn't. *Oh.* She…had…*not*—and the minute the door had closed behind them they had been all over each other.

Their first kiss had been hungry—almost clumsy. They'd reached blindly for each other in the hall as some ornament had gone crashing to the ground, and he'd ended up pushing her up against the wall with his hand halfway up her dress until he'd realised that he hadn't wanted to do it to her like that. Not on her wedding night. Not after last time. He wanted to show her he knew the meaning of the word *consideration*. He wanted to make love to her slowly—very slowly. And so she had allowed him to lead her to his bedroom where now she stood, looking around her with a slightly nervous expression on her face.

'I suppose this must be the scene of a thousand seductions?'

'A rather inflated estimate,' he responded drily.

'You don't want me to lie to you? To say you're the first woman I've brought here?'

She gave a funny little smile. 'No, of course not.'

'I haven't asked you about any of *your* former lovers, have I?'

'No, that's right. You haven't.'

He wondered what he was trying to do—whether he was trying to sabotage things before they'd even got started. Why the hell hadn't he just told her that in her silvery gown she eclipsed every other woman he'd ever known? That she was beautiful and soft and completely desirable? With a small growl of anger directed mainly at himself, he pulled her into his arms and kissed her again and he heard the gasping little sound she made as she caught hold of his shoulders. He kissed her for a long time, until she started to relax—until she began to press herself against his body and the barrier of their clothes suddenly seemed like something he couldn't endure for a second longer. He led her over to the bed and sat her down on the edge, before getting down on his knees in front of her.

'What are you doing?' she joked weakly as he began to unstrap one of her shoes. 'You've already made the proposal.'

He lifted his gaze; his expression mocking. 'I thought it was you who did the proposing?'

'Oh, yes.' She tipped her head back and expelled a breath as he started rubbing the pad of his thumb over her instep. 'So I did.'

He removed both shoes and peeled off her silvery wedding dress before laying her back on the bed and kicking off his shoes and socks. He lay down next to her, pushing the hair from her face and brushing his lips over hers, taking his time. 'You are very beautiful,' he said.

'I'm—'

He silenced her with the press of his forefinger over her mouth. 'The correct response is, thank you, Alek.'

She swallowed. 'Thank you, Alek.'

'But I'm afraid of hurting you.'

She reached her hand up to brush a strand

of hair off his forehead and suddenly her face looked very tender. He felt his heart clench.

'Because of the baby?' she asked softly.

He nodded, still wary around that shining tenderness which instinctively put him on his guard. 'Because of the baby,' he repeated.

'The doctor said it was okay.' She leant forward and kissed him. 'But that maybe we should avoid swinging from the chandeliers.'

'I don't have any…chandeliers,' he said indistinctly, but suddenly the flirting word games of foreplay became swamped by a far more primitive need to possess. Refocusing his attention, he began to explore her properly—touching the coolness of her flesh above her stocking tops as she began to make soft little sounds of pleasure. Did she feel his uncharacteristic hesitation as his fingers tiptoed upwards? Could she hear the loud pounding of his heart? Did she know that suddenly—ridiculously—this felt completely new?

'It's no different from how it was before,' she whispered. 'I'm still me.'

He kissed her again. But it *was* different. She

was like a ship carrying a precious cargo. His baby. He swallowed as his finger trailed over her navel and he could tell she was holding her breath, expelling it only when he eased his hand beneath the elastic of her panties and cupped her where she was warm and wet.

'Oh,' she said.

His mouth hovered over hers. 'Oh,' he echoed indistinctly as, blindly, he reached for his belt and suddenly she was unbuttoning his shirt, making a low sound of pleasure as she slipped it away from his shoulders. And he stopped thinking. He just gave himself up to every erotic second. There was a snap as he released her bra and her breasts tumbled into his eager hands. He felt the slide of her bare thigh against his as she used her foot to push his trousers down his legs. He could smell the musky aroma of her sex as he peeled off her panties and threw them aside.

Their eyes met in a long moment and he felt shaken by the sudden unexpected intimacy of that.

He slid the flat of his hand over her hip. 'I don't want to hurt you—'

She bit her lip, as if she was about to say something controversial but had thought better of it at the last moment. 'Just make love to me, Alek,' she said with a simple sincerity which tore through him like a flame.

Slowly he eased himself inside her, uttering something guttural in Greek, which wasn't like him. But none of this was *like* him. He'd never felt this close to a woman before, nor so aware of her as a person rather than as just a body. It rocked him to the core and, yes, it intimidated him, too—and he didn't like that. He wasn't used to being out of control. To feeling as if he were putty in a woman's hands. He groaned. Maybe not putty. Because putty was soft, wasn't it? And he was hard. Ah, *neh*. He was very hard. Harder than he could ever remember. And if he wasn't careful, he was going to come too soon.

This is sex, he told himself fiercely. *Sex which you both want. So treat it like sex.* Breaking eye contact, he buried his face in her neck as he began to take command, each slow and deliberate thrust demonstrating his power and control.

He smiled against her skin when she moaned his name and smiled some more when she began to gasp in a rising crescendo. 'Oh, yes...*yes*!'

He raised his head and watched as she came. Saw her tip her head back and her eyes close. He saw her body shudder and heard the disbelieving little cry which followed. And then he saw the first big fat tear which rolled down her cheek to be quickly followed by another, and he frowned. Because hadn't she cried last time—and wasn't the deal supposed to be that this time there were no tears? No regrets. His mouth twisted. No nothing—only pleasure.

'Alek,' she whispered and he could no longer hold back—letting go in a great burst of seed which pumped from his body as if it was never going to stop.

He must have fallen asleep, and when eventually he opened his eyes again he found her sleeping, too. Rolling away, he stared up at the ceiling, but although his heart was still pounding with post-orgasmic euphoria he felt confusion slide a cold and bewildering trail across his skin.

He glanced around the room. Her wedding dress lay on the floor along with his own discarded trousers and shirt. His usually pristine bedroom looked as if someone had ransacked it and he found himself remembering the ornament breaking in the hall—a priceless piece of porcelain shattered into a hundred pieces which had crunched beneath his feet.

What was it about her which made him lose control like that? He turned his head to look at her again—a pale Venus rising from the crumpled white waves of the sheets. His gaze shifted to her belly—still flat—and his heart clenched as he thought about the reality of being a father.

The fears he'd been trying to silence now crowded darkly in his mind. What if certain traits were inherited rather than learnt? Wasn't that one of the reasons why he'd always ruled out fatherhood as a life choice, not daring to take the risk of failing as miserably at the task as his own father had done?

She began to stir and opened her eyes and he

thought how bright and clear they looked, with no hint of tears now.

'Why do you cry?' he asked suddenly. 'When I make love to you?'

Ellie brushed her fringe out of her eyes, more as a stalling mechanism than anything else. His question suggested a layer of intimacy she hadn't been expecting and that surprised her. This was supposed to be about sex, wasn't it? That was what she thought his agenda was. The only agenda there could possibly be—no matter what her feelings for him were. If she suddenly came out and told him the reason she'd cried was because he made her feel *complete*, then wouldn't he laugh, or run screaming in the opposite direction? If she told him that when he was deep inside her, it felt as if she'd been waiting her whole life for that moment, wouldn't it come over as fanciful, or—worse—needy? If she told him she was crying for all the things she would never have from him—like his *love*—wouldn't that make her seem like just another woman greedily trying to take from him something she knew he would never give?

She told him part of the truth. 'Because you are an amazing lover.'

'And that makes you cry?'

'Blame my hormones.'

'I suppose I should be flattered,' he drawled. 'Though, of course, that would depend on how experienced you are.'

She pushed her hair out of her eyes and narrowed her eyes. 'Are you fishing to find out how many lovers I've had before you?'

'Is it unreasonable of me to want to know?'

She sat up and looked down at his dark body outlined against the tumbled bedding. 'I've had one long-term relationship before this and that's all I'm going to say on the subject, because I think it's distasteful to discuss it, especially at a time like this. Is that acceptable?'

'Completely acceptable would be for there to have been no one before me.' He smiled, but it was a smile tinged with intent rather than humour. 'And since I intend to drive the memory of anyone else from your mind for ever, you'd better come back over here and kiss me right now.'

His hand starfished over her breast and, even though his questioning was unfair and his attitude outrageously macho, Ellie couldn't seem to stop herself from reacting to him. She wondered what he'd say if she told him he'd banished every other man from her mind the first time he'd kissed her. Would he be surprised? Probably not. Women probably told him that kind of thing all the time.

It hadn't been her plan to have him parting her legs again quite so soon, and certainly not to cry his name out like a kind of prayer as he entered her a second time. But she did. And afterwards she was left feeling exposed and naked in all kinds of ways, while he remained as much of an enigma as he'd always done.

She lay there wrapped in his arms and although his lips pressing against her shoulder were making his words muffled, they were still clear enough to hear.

'I'm thinking that we ought to start sleeping

together from now on—what about you?' he said. 'Because it would be crazy not to.'

It was a strangely emotionless conclusion to their lovemaking and Ellie didn't know why she was so disappointed, because he was only behaving true to form. But she made sure her smile didn't slip and show her disappointment. She kept her expression as neutral as his. He wanted to treat sex as simply another appetite to be fed, did he?

Well, then, so would she.

She lay back against the pillow and coiled her arms around his neck. 'Absolutely crazy,' she agreed huskily.

CHAPTER TEN

HER WEDDING RING no longer mocked her and neither did the closed door of Alek's room. Because Ellie now shared that room, just as she shared the bed within and the man who slept in it.

Pulling on a tea dress, Ellie began to brush her hair. To all intents and purposes, she and Alek now had a 'full' marriage. Ever since the night of their wedding—when they'd broken the sexual drought—they had been enjoying the pleasures of the marital bed in a way which had surpassed her every expectation.

He could turn her on with a single smile. He could have her naked in his arms in seconds. Even when she told herself she ought to resist him—in a futile attempt to regain some control over her shattered equilibrium—she would fail time and time again.

'But you can't resist me, *poulaki mou*,' he would murmur, as if he guessed exactly what she was trying to do. 'You know you really want me.'

And that was the trouble. She did. She couldn't seem to stop wanting him, no matter how much she tried to tell herself that she was getting in too deep. And if sometimes she lay looking wistfully at the ceiling after he'd made love to her, she made sure it was while Alek was asleep. She tried to stop herself from caring for him too much—and certainly to hide her feelings for him. Because that wasn't what he wanted. This was as close to a business arrangement as a personal relationship could be.

But her life had changed in other ways, too. They started going out more as a couple, so that at times the marriage felt almost authentic. He took her to the theatre, which she loved. They watched films and ate in fancy restaurants and explored all the tiny backstreets of the city. They drove down to the south coast, to visit Luis and Carly in their amazing house which overlooked a beautiful river.

And yet, despite the increased richness of their day-to-day existence, it was difficult to get to know the real man behind the steely image, despite the external thaw between them. He could do that thoughtful stuff of massaging her feet when she was tired, but if his fingers hadn't been made of flesh and blood she might have thought she was being administered to by some sort of robot. Sometimes it felt as if she didn't know him any better than when that list of his likes and dislikes had been circulated to staff at The Hog before his arrival. She still wasn't sure what motivated him, or what made him sometimes wake her in the night when he'd had a dream which had clearly been a bad one. She would turn to find his eyes open but not really seeing, his body tense—suspended between the two worlds of sleeping and waking. But when she gently shook him awake, his face would become guarded and he would deflect her concerns with something sensual enough to send any questions scuttling from her mind.

He was a master at concealing the real man

who lay beneath; adept at avoiding questions. His cool blue eyes would narrow if she tried to probe more deeply; his gaze becoming one of sapphire ice. *Don't push me*, those eyes seemed to say. But that didn't stop Ellie from trying, even though he would deflect her questions by sliding his hand beneath her skirt and starting to make love to her. He'd leave her breathless and panting as all her questions dissolved and nothing was left but the pleasure he gave her, time after time. And she didn't give up. She just lowered her sights a little. She stopped expecting big revelations and just concentrated on the little ones.

And every time she discovered something about him, it felt like a major victory—like another little missing bit of the jigsaw. In those sleepy moments after making love, he told her about how he'd worked his way up from being a kitchen boy in Athens, to owning an entire chain of restaurants. He told her about working on a fancy vineyard in California, so that he knew all about the wine trade. He made a wistful face when he described his friend Murat's beautiful country of Qurhah and told her how big the stars looked when you were out in the middle of the desert. He explained how life was just one great big learning experience and everything he knew, he had taught himself.

And one thing she was learning faster than any other was that it wasn't so easy to put the brakes on her own emotions. She wasn't sure if it was her fluctuating hormones which were changing her feelings towards her Greek husband, or just that sex had removed the protective shield from her heart. No matter how hard she tried, she couldn't seem to stop herself from caring for him in a way that went bone-deep. Her heart was stubbornly refusing to listen to all the logic her head tried to throw at it.

Yet she *knew* what happened to women who were stupid enough to love men who didn't love them back. She'd watched her mother's life become diminished because she had wanted something she was never going to have. She'd wasted years on bitterness and resentment, because she'd

refused to accept that you couldn't make another
person do what you wanted them to.

And that was not going to happen to her.
She wouldn't let it.

Smoothing down the folds of her tea dress, she
walked into the kitchen to find Alek seated at
the table, a half-full coffee pot beside him as he
worked his way through a stack of financial newspapers. He glanced up as she walked in, his eyes
following her every step, like a snake bewitched
by a charmer. She had become used to his very
macho appraisal of her appearance and, with a
certain amount of guilt, had grown to enjoy it.

He put the newspaper down as she sat down
opposite him and his eyes glinted as she reached
for the honeypot.

'I enjoyed licking my favourite honey last
night,' he murmured.

Her eyes widened. 'Alek!'

'Are you blushing, Ellie?'

'Certainly not. It's just the steam from the coffee making me hot.'

'Would you like to come to Italy?' he questioned.

Ellie dropped the little wooden spatula back in the pot. 'You mean, with you?' she said.

'Of course with me. Unless you had someone else in mind?' He smiled and gave a lazy shrug. 'We can treat it as a kind of honeymoon, if you like. I thought we could go to Lucca. I have business in Pisa and I can go there afterwards while you fly home. And Lucca is an extraordinarily pretty city. They call it the hidden gem of Tuscany. It has an oval piazza instead of a square one and a tower with trees growing out of the top. Lots of dark and winding streets and iconic churches. You've never been there?'

She shook her head. 'I've never been anywhere apart from a day trip to Calais with my mother.'

'Well, then.' He raised his eyebrows. 'Didn't you once tell me how much you longed to travel?'

Yes, she'd told him that, but that had been when she'd still had ambition burning big in her heart. When travelling had been part of her work plan and independence had been a believable dream which seemed to have fallen by the wayside since she'd discovered she was pregnant. She thought of Italy—with its green hills and terracotta roofs. All those famous churches and marble statues she'd only ever seen in pictures.

Wouldn't it be good to go on an unexpected honeymoon for some sunshine and culture—even if it was the most unconventional honeymoon in the history of the world? And yet, just the fact that Alek had suggested it brightened her mood. Wasn't this a bit of a breakthrough from her enigmatic husband? Could she possibly make it a *real* honeymoon—as if they were people who genuinely cared about one another, rather than two people who were just trying to make the best of a bad situation?

She began to spread the thick, golden honey on her toast and smiled at him. 'I'd like that,' she said. 'I'd like that very much.'

'*Thavmassios*. We will fly the day after tomorrow.'

Two days later their flight touched down in Pisa where Alek had arranged for a car to take them to Lucca. The drive took less than an hour and they arrived in the late afternoon, when all the shops were closed and the place had a drowsy feel about it. Ellie looked up at the high city walls and thought she'd never seen anywhere more beautiful. Alek had rented an old-fashioned apartment overlooking a sheltered courtyard, where geraniums tumbled brightly from terracotta pots. The wooden frame of their bed was dark and worn and the sheets were crisp and scented with lavender.

She knew that they weren't like other traditional honeymooners, and yet as he closed the apartment door behind them Ellie was filled with something which felt awfully like *hope*. She thought: *We're in a city where nobody knows us. Two strangers blending with all the other strangers.* Mightn't there be a chance that here the man she had married would let his mask slip for once, when there was only her to see?

They made love, unpacked and showered and then Alek took her out to dinner in a garden shimmering with candlelight where they ate the local delicacy of *tortelli lucchese*—a bright yellow stuffed pasta, topped with a rich ragu sauce. Afterwards, they sat beneath the star-spangled sky and drank their coffee—their fingers linking together on the table, and for once it felt real. As if they really were genuine honeymooners and not just a pair of actors acting out the parts. When he took her home, she put her arms around his neck and kissed him passionately and he picked her up and carried her to the bedroom with a look on his face which made her tremble.

The following morning Ellie awoke alone. For a minute she lay there as sensual memories of the previous night filtered into her mind, then she pulled on a robe, splashed cold water over her sleepy face and went off to find Alek. He was sitting on their balcony with breakfast laid out on the small table and the aroma of coffee vying with the powerful scent of jasmine.

'Where did all this come from?' she questioned as she looked at the crisp bread, the buttery pastries and the rich red jam.

'I got up early and you looked much too peaceful to wake. I went for a walk around the city walls and called in at the *panificio* on the way back.' He poured out two cups of coffee and pushed one across the table and smiled. 'So what would you like to do today?'

And suddenly—she had no idea what caused it—the perfect scene before her began to disintegrate. It was like tugging at a tiny nick on a delicate piece of fabric which suddenly ripped open. It all seemed so *false*. There was Alek—looking ruggedly handsome in an open-necked white shirt and dark trousers, his blue eyes gleaming like jewels. Yet his polite distance made her feel as if she were just another item to be ticked off on his agenda. His smile seemed more automatic than genuine and she found herself resenting his control and his inbuilt detachment. *This has nothing to do with reality*, she thought, as a feeling of rebellion began to bubble up inside her.

She sat down and looked at him. 'Actually, I'd like to talk about the baby.'

He stilled. 'The baby?'

'That's right. Our baby. You know. The one we never talk about.' She paused and laid her hand

over her stomach. 'Because although it's growing inside me, we never discuss it, do we? We
always seem to skirt around the subject. I mean,
I go to the doctor and report back with a clean
bill of health—and you manage to look pleased.
And once or twice you've even come with me
and you nod your head in all the right places,
but you still act like nothing's happening, or as
if it's happening to someone else. As if none of
this is real.'

A shuttered look came over his face and he
shrugged. 'I suppose we could sit around having hypothetical discussions about what we're
going to do and how we're going to react when
the baby arrives, but why bother when it's impossible to predict?'

'So you just want to ignore it until it happens?'

His eyes became hooded and suddenly he didn't
look quite so detached. 'Isn't that what I've just
said?'

And Ellie heard the distortion in his words—
the crack of bitterness he couldn't quite hide.
She saw the way his body had grown hard and

tense and wondered what had caused it. And she wondered why she didn't have the guts to come right out and ask him, and keep on asking him until he finally gave her an answer. What was she so afraid of? Scared that if she unlocked his secrets, she'd discover something to kill off the dormant hope which lingered so foolishly in her heart? Surely it was better to know and to face up to the truth, no matter how grim it was... Better that than building dreams which were never going to materialise.

'You know, through all the time we've been together, you've never spoken about your childhood,' she said. 'Apart from a throwaway comment about never having used public transport because your father owned an island.'

'And why do you think that is?' he questioned. 'If somebody doesn't want to talk about something, there's usually a reason why.'

'You've never told me anything about your family,' she continued stubbornly. 'Not a single thing. I don't even know if you've got any brothers or sisters—'

'I don't.'

'And you've never mentioned your parents.'

Unsmilingly, he looked into her eyes. 'Maybe that's because I don't want to.'

'Alek.' She leant forward. 'You need to tell me.'

'Why?' he snapped.

'Because this baby is going to share your parents' genes. Your father—'

'Is dead,' he said flatly. 'And believe me, you'd better hope that our baby doesn't share many of his genes.'

A shiver ran down her spine. 'And what about your mother?'

For a moment there was silence. 'What about her?'

Ellie was unprepared for the savage note in his voice or the bunching of his powerful shoulders. Everything about his reaction told her she was entering dangerous territory—but she knew she couldn't let up. Not this time. If she backtracked now she might win his temporary approval, but then what? She would simply be signing up to a life of half-truths. Bringing up a baby in a world of ignorance, where nothing was what it really seemed. Because knowledge was power. *And wasn't the balance of power in this relationship already hopelessly unequal?*

'Is she still alive?'

'I don't know,' he snapped, his voice as cold as ice. 'I don't know a damned thing about her. Do you want me to spell it out for you in words of one syllable, Ellie? She walked out on me when I was a baby. And while I'm known for my amazing sense of recall—not even I can remember that. Are you satisfied now?'

Ellie's head was spinning. *His mother had walked out on him.* Wasn't that the worst thing that could happen to someone? Hadn't she read somewhere that it was better to be abused than abandoned, and wondered at the time if that was true? She supposed you could always challenge your abuser—but if you were deserted, wouldn't that leave you with no choice except to feel empty and bewildered? She imagined a tiny baby waking up one morning crying for his mother—only that mother never came. How would that feel, to miss the comfort of a maternal embrace and never know it again? Even if the bond wasn't strong, a cuddle would still feel like safety to a helpless infant. On some primitive and subliminal level—would that make it impossible for you to put your trust in a woman afterwards? Would that explain his coldness and his lack of real intimacy, no matter how many times they had sex?

'What…what happened?'

'I just told you.'

'But you didn't.' She met his gaze, determined not to be cowed by the fury sparking from those cold blue depths. 'You only gave me the bare facts.'

'And didn't it occur to you that maybe that's all I wanted to give you?' Pushing back his chair, he got up from the table and began to pace around the veranda like a man in a cell. 'Why don't you learn when enough is enough?'

She'd never seen him so angry and a few weeks ago Ellie might have backed down, but not any more. She wasn't someone who was trying to win his affection or keep the peace, no matter what. She was a mother-to-be and she wanted to be the best mother she possibly could be—and that meant decoding her baby's father, even if he didn't want her to. Even if it pushed them further apart, it was a risk she had to take.

'Because it's not enough,' she said stubbornly.

'What difference does it make that a woman walked out of a house on a Greek island over thirty years ago?'

'It makes all kinds of difference. I want to know about *her*. I want to know whether she was artistic, or good at math. I'm trying to join up all the dots, Alek—to imagine what kind of characteristics our baby might inherit. Maybe it's extra important to me because I don't know much about my own father. If things were different, I'd have learnt the answers to some of these questions already.'

Alek stared at her as her passionate words broke into the quiet Italian morning. Her own upbringing hadn't been much of a picnic but, despite all that, her mother had stuck by her, hadn't she? Ellie hadn't been rejected by the one person you were supposed to be able to rely on. Behind her the jasmine and miniature lemon trees made her look like a character in a painting. In her silky robe she looked fresh and young, and nothing could disguise the flicker of hope in her eyes. Did she think there was going to be some fairy-tale ending, that he could soothe everything over and make everything okay with a few carefully chosen words?

His jaw tightened. Maybe he *should* tell her the truth. Let her understand the kind of man he really was—and why. Let her know that his emotional coldness wasn't something he'd just invented to pass the time. It had been ground into him from the start—embedded too deeply for him to be any other way. Maybe knowing that would nip any rosy dreams she was in danger of nurturing. Show her why the barriers he'd erected around himself were impenetrable. *And why he wouldn't want them any other way.*

'There were no custody visits or vacations,' he said. 'For a long time, I knew nothing about my mother. Or indeed, any mother. When you grow up without something, you don't even re-alise you're missing it. Her name was never men-tioned in front of me, and the only women I knew were my father's whores.'

She flinched at his use of the word and he saw her compose her face into an expression of un-derstanding. 'It's perfectly reasonable not to like the women who supplanted your mother—'

'Oh, please. Quit the amateur psychology,' he interrupted, pushing his fingers impatiently through his hair. 'I'm not making a prudish judge-ment because it makes me feel better. They *were* whores. They looked like whores and acted like whores. He paid them for sex. They were the only women I came in contact with. I grew up think-ing that all females caked their face in make-up and wore skirts short enough for you to see their knickers.' And one in particular who had invited a boy of twelve to take her knickers down so that she could *show him a good time.*

Did she believe him now? Was that why she was biting her lip? He could almost see her mind working overtime as she searched for something to say—as if trying to find a positive spin to put on what he'd just told her. He could have saved her the trouble and told her there was none.

'But…you must have had friends,' she said, a touch of desperation in her voice now. 'You must have looked at *their* mothers, and wondered what had happened to yours.'

'I had no friends,' he said flatly. 'My life was carefully controlled. I might as well have had a prison as a house. I saw no one except for the servants—my father liked childless, unmarried servants who could devote all their time to him. And if you have nothing with which to compare, then no comparisons can be made. His island was remote and inaccessible. He ran everything and owned everything. I lived in a vast complex which was more like a palace and I was tutored at home. I didn't find out anything about my mother until I was seven years old and when I did—the boy who told me was beaten.'

He stared into space. Should he tell her that the boy's injuries had been so bad that he'd been airlifted to the hospital on the mainland and had never returned? And that the boy's parents—even though they had been extremely poor—had threatened to go to the police? Alek had only been young but he remembered the panic which had swirled around the complex as a result. He remembered the fearful faces of his father's aides, as if the old man really *had* overstepped the mark this time. But he'd wriggled out of it, just as he always did. Money had been offered, and accepted. Money got you whatever it was you wanted. It bought silence as well as sex—and another catastrophe had been averted. *And hadn't he done that, too? Hadn't he paid off Ellie's contract with the Irishwoman with the same ruthlessness which his father would have employed?*

He saw the distress on her face and tried to imagine how this must sound through her ears. Incredible, probably. Like one of those porn films his father's bodyguards used to watch, late into the night. He wondered if he stopped the story now, whether it would be enough to make her understand why he was not like other men. But she had demanded the truth and perhaps she would

continue to demand it. To niggle away at it, as
women invariably did. He realised that for the
first time in his life he couldn't just block her out,
or refuse to take her calls. To fade her into the
background as if she had never existed, which
was what he'd always done before. Whether he
liked it or not, he was stuck with Ellie Brooks, or
Ellie Sarantos as she was now. And maybe she
ought to learn that it was better not to ask questions in case you didn't like the answers.

'Anything else you want to know?' he demanded. 'Any other stone you've left unturned?'

'What did the boy tell you about your mother?'

'He told me the truth. That she'd left in the
middle of the night with one of the island's
fishermen.' He leant back against the intricate
wrought-iron tracings of the balustrade. Somewhere in the distance he could hear a woman
call out in Italian and a child answered. 'It was
convenient that she chose a lover with his own
boat, for there would have been no other way of
her leaving the island without my father knowing
about it. But I guess her main achievement was

in managing to conduct an affair right under his nose, without the old man finding out. And the fact that she was prepared to risk his rage.' His mouth twisted. 'She must have been quite some woman.'

He felt a pain he hadn't felt in a long time. A hot, unwelcome pain which excluded everything else. It stabbed at his heart like a rusty knife and he wished he'd told her to mind her own business, but now he was on a roll and somehow he couldn't stop—pain or no pain. 'My father was completely humiliated by her desertion and determined to wipe away all traces of her. Something he found surprisingly easy to accomplish.' He looked into her bright eyes and then he said it. He'd never admitted it before. Never told anyone. Not the therapist he'd half-heartedly consulted when he'd been living in New York, not any of his friends, nor the women who'd shared his bed in the intervening years and tried to dig away to get at the truth. No one. Not until now. He swallowed as the bitterness rose up inside him like a dark tide. 'I never even saw a photo of her. He destroyed them all. My mother is a stranger to me. I don't even know what she looks like.'

She didn't gasp or utter some meaningless platitude. She just sat there and nodded—as if she was absorbing everything he'd told her. 'But... didn't you ever think about tracking her down and hearing her side of the story?'

He stared at her. 'Why would I want to find a woman who left me behind?'

'Oh, Alek. Because she's your mum, that's why.' She got up and walked across the sun-dappled balcony until she'd reached him. And then she put her arms tightly around his back and held him, as if she never wanted to let him go.

He felt her fingers wrapping themselves around him—like one of those speeded-up documentaries of a fast-growing vine which covered everything in seconds. He tried to move away. He didn't need her softness or her sympathy. He didn't need a thing from her. He had learnt to live with pain and abandonment and to normalise them. He had pushed his memories into a place of restricted access and had slammed the door on them…what right did she have to make him open the door and stare at all those dark spectres? Did she get some kind of *kick* out of making him confront stuff that was dead and buried?

He wanted to push her away, but her soft body was melting against his. Her fingers were burying themselves in his hair and suddenly he was kissing her like a man who had finally lost control. Losing himself in a kiss as sweet as honey and being sucked into a sensation which was making him feel…

He jerked away from her, his heart pounding. He didn't want to *feel* anything. She'd stirred up stuff which was better left alone and she needed to learn that he was not prepared to tolerate such an intrusion. She'd done it once, but it would not happen again. With an effort, he steadied his breath.

'I don't really want to provide some sort of erotic floor show for the surrounding apartments,' he said, his voice cold as he walked over to the table and poured himself a glass of juice. 'So why don't you sit down and eat your breakfast, before we start sightseeing? You wanted to travel, didn't you, Ellie? Better not waste this golden opportunity.'

CHAPTER ELEVEN

IT WAS NOT a successful honeymoon.

Yes, Lucca was completely gorgeous, and, with her brand-new sun hat crammed down over her hair, Ellie accompanied Alek to every iconic destination the beautiful city had to offer. She saw the tower with the trees growing from the top and drank cappuccino in the famous oval piazza. They visited so many churches that she lost count, and ate their meals in leafy squares and hidden courtyards. There were marble statues in beautiful gardens, where roses grew beside lemon trees. And when the sun became too fierce there were shady streets to walk down, with the rich smell of leather purses and handbags wafting out from the tiny shops which lined them.

But a new *froideur* had settled over Alek. It didn't seem to matter that her first instincts on meeting him had been correct—and that on some level they *were* kindred spirits. They'd both known pretty awful childhoods but had just chosen to deal with them in different ways. And yes, she'd managed at last to extract the truth about his past. She now knew him better…but at what price? It hadn't made them closer, or brought them together in some magical kind of way.

It was as if the confidences she'd forced him to share had ruptured the tentative truce which had existed between them. As if he'd closed right down and shut her out—only this time she sensed there was no going back. No chink of light coming from behind the steely door he had retreated behind. The anger had gone and in its place was a consideration and cool courtesy which made him seem even further away. He spoke to her as if he were her doctor. Was she too hot? Too tired? A little hungry, perhaps? And she would assure him that she felt absolutely fine, because what was the alternative?

But she didn't feel fine. She felt headachey and out of sorts—with a kind of heaviness which seemed to have entered her limbs and which she put down to the new tension which had sprung up between them. She understood now why he was emotionally distant, but she still didn't know how to solve it.

Vasos called several times from London but instead of saying something like, *sorry, but I'm on my honeymoon*—Alek took every call and spent as much time as possible on it. Or so it seemed to Ellie. She would be left sitting on the terrace, her book stuck on the same page while he spoke in a torrent of Greek she couldn't understand.

She stared at the unread pages of her novel. Had she thought this was going to be easy? Had she been naive enough to think that extracting information about his painful childhood might make him warm and open towards her? If she'd known that the opposite would be true, she might have thought twice before quizzing him about the mother who had deserted him. She slammed the book shut. No wonder he was so closed off. So lacklustre about *their* baby.

Feeling queasy, she glanced up to see him

standing framed by the miniature orange trees which grew on their leafy terrace and frowning as he slid his cell phone back into his pocket.

'That was Vasos,' he said.

'Again?'

'The new deal on the Rafael building seems to be nearing completion earlier than planned and the architect is flying into London later this evening.'

'And let me guess.' Her voice was light. 'You need to get back?'

'I'm afraid I do. My business in Pisa will have to wait.' His frown deepened as he seemed to look at her properly for the first time. 'You're sweating, Ellie. Are you okay?'

No, she was not okay. She felt hot and dizzy and disillusioned. Maybe it was time to stop grabbing at rainbows and settle for reality.

'I'm fine,' she said tightly. 'I'd better go and pack.'

Something dark and unwanted rose up inside him as Alek watched her go, her shoulders tight with tension. Something which clutched at his heart and made it twist with pain. *Damn her*, he thought. Why hadn't he slapped her down? Why hadn't he refused to answer all those intrusive questions which had done nothing but open up a dark can of worms?

And yet now that he had pushed her away, the sense of relief he'd been anticipating hadn't happened. They'd been doing that thing of sleeping on opposite sides of the bed—their breathing sounding unnaturally loud in the darkness of the night—each knowing the other was awake and yet not speaking. *Because they had nothing left to say.*

Was it some cruel twist of fate which had left him feeling so lost without the softness of her arms around him? A taunting reminder of just how empty and alone rejection could make you feel. And yet wasn't it better this way? For him to do the rejecting rather than risk being pushed away for a second time?

When she returned from packing, he thought her face looked almost translucent beneath the brim of her straw hat, which she had worn during most of the trip. The Italian sun had barely touched her skin and her grey eyes seemed shadowed, and even though he knew he ought to say something he could think of nothing which would fall easily into the empty silence. She was quiet all during the journey back to London and the moment their plane touched down and he turned on his phone, it began to vibrate with a flurry of calls. And deep down, wasn't he glad to have the opportunity to lose himself in the infinitely more straightforward problems of work? Far better than having to confront the silent reproach or the lip she kept biting as if she was trying to hold back tears. He had the car drop her off at the apartment while he went straight to the office.

'You don't mind?' he questioned.

She gave an unconvincing laugh, as if she recognised the question for what it was—a meaningless platitude. 'And if I do? Would you be prepared to put your precious work aside and spend the afternoon with me, if I asked you to?'

'Ellie—'

'I'll take that as a no,' she said with another

brittle smile. 'Anyway, I want to have a lie-down. I'm tired.'

After he'd gone she closed the bedroom curtains and, switching her phone to Silent, left it in her handbag on the far side of the room. But she could hear it vibrating like a persistent fly as she lay on the bed drifting in and out of an uncomfortable doze—too lazy to get up and switch it off completely.

By five o'clock she forced herself to get up and saw there were three missed calls from a number she didn't recognise. Muzzily, she took a shower but her mood was still flat as she pulled on a pair of linen trousers and a T-shirt. She was drinking a glass of water when the doorbell rang.

Touching her fingertips to her belly, she went to answer the door to find a blonde woman standing on the step—someone she didn't recognise but who looked oddly familiar.

'Can I help you?' questioned Ellie.

'You don't remember me?'

Ellie shook her head. 'Should I?'

'Probably. I knew you before you were married.

I was staying at The Hog when you were working there. Remember now?'

And suddenly the mist cleared. Of course. It was the journalist. The sneaky blonde who had asked those questions which Ellie had stupidly answered, and which had ended up with her getting the sack. She looked into the woman's glacial eyes.

'I've got nothing to say to you,' said Ellie.

'Maybe not. But you might be interested in what I have to say to you.'

'I don't think so.' She started to close the door. 'My husband doesn't like journalists and neither do I.'

'Does your husband realise he has a brother?'

Sweat broke out on her forehead as Ellie leant against the door. She thought about what Alek had told her about his childhood. And amid all the pain and the heartbreak of his upbringing, he hadn't mentioned his father having any more children. *But maybe his mother had gone on to have more children. If he'd never met her, he wouldn't actually know, would he?* 'You're lying,' she croaked.

'Why would I lie? Actually, he has a *twin* brother. Yeah, I thought you'd be interested.'

Yes, she was interested but that didn't stop Ellie from shaking her head, because the dramatic words seemed to make no sense. 'But if what you say is true, how come you know and he doesn't?'

The woman shrugged. 'His brother asked me to track him down and speak to him. He wanted to know whether Alek would be receptive to a meeting. The first part wasn't difficult but the second part was, because I could never get close enough to ask him. Men like Alek Sarantos are never easy to get close to. He doesn't do interviews and he's not the kind of man who drinks alone in bars, so trying to pick him up was never going to work. And as you say, he doesn't like journalists.'

'Are you surprised?'

'Nothing surprises me any more,' said the woman cynically. 'That's why I couldn't believe my luck when I saw him with you that night. A waitress who was way out of his league and you were making out like two teenagers at a school disco! I thought I had the perfect opportunity to smoke him out, and I was right.'

'Smoke him out?' echoed Ellie in horror.

'Sure. Put a woman into a man's life and immediately you've got another way in.'

'You're disgusting.'

'No, honey. I'm just doing my job.' The journalist leant forward and tucked a business card into Ellie's free hand. 'Why don't you tell him to call me?'

After she'd gone, Ellie shut the door, leaning back against it and trying very hard to steady her breathing.

A brother.

A *twin* brother.

How could that be? Did Alek know about this explosive fact and was this just one more thing he had deliberately omitted to tell her? She felt so spaced out that she couldn't seem to take it in. Had the journalist being doing what journalists did so well…inventing a story to try to get some sort of reaction? Her heart was pounding and a weird kind of pain was spearing through her and she wasn't sure how long she stood there, only that she couldn't stay there. She couldn't let Alek come home from work and find her slumped there like a zombie.

She forced herself to dress, but the silky tea dress seemed only to mock her. She remembered the day she'd gone shopping, when she'd felt so proud of herself. So stupidly proud. As if managing to run up a massive bill on a man's credit card all by herself was some sort of mega achievement. She remembered how easy she'd found it to spend his money. For all her feisty words, was she really any different from the other women who adored his wealth? He hated gold-diggers. He seemed to hate women in general and now she could understand why.

Never had that famous saying seemed more appropriate.

Give me the child until he is seven and I will give you the man.

Wasn't that just the truth?

Alek had spent the first years of his life deserted by his mother and left alone with a cruel father. Was it any wonder that he'd locked his emotions away and thrown away the key?

She got more and more nervy as time wore on but when eventually Alek arrived home and walked into the sitting room, she thought how weary he looked. She'd been intending to break it to him gently but maybe something in her expression alerted him, because he frowned the minute he saw her.

'What's wrong?'

She'd been racking her brain to come up with the right way of telling him, but maybe there was no *right* way. There were only facts. She couldn't protect him from what she was about to tell him, no matter how much she wanted to.

'You remember that journalist who wrote the diary piece about us?'

He tensed. 'I'm not likely to forget her.'

'Well, she was here today.'

He scowled. 'How the hell did she find out where I lived?'

'I don't think that's really the issue here.'

'No?' His mouth twisted. 'Well, my privacy *is* an issue, something which I thought you might have realised by now. What did you tell her this time?' He gave a bitter laugh. 'Did you give her a blow-by-blow account of your husband's tragic childhood?'

'I would *never*—'

'Or maybe you thought you'd announce the baby news.' His words cut over hers. 'Even though we agreed not to say anything before the twelve weeks is up?'

'Actually, she was the one with the news.' She hesitated and then drew a deep breath. 'She told me that you've got a brother.'

His eyes narrowed. 'What the hell are you talking about?'

'Actually, a twin brother.' She licked her lips. 'You didn't know?'

'I don't know what you're talking about,' he said coldly.

'He asked her to contact you, to see if you'd be receptive to a meeting.'

'I do not have a brother!' he thundered.

'Alek...' But her words were forgotten as her body was racked by the most piercing pain Ellie had ever felt. Hot knives were chasing through her belly and stabbing deeper and deeper. All the strength was draining from her legs. Shakily, she reached out to grab the edge of the window seat as Alek strode across the room, his face criss-crossed with concern as he caught hold of her.

But she didn't want his concern. She just wanted something to stop the pain. Not just the one in her belly—but the one in her heart.

'Go away!' she mumbled, lashing out at him ineffectively—but she could see something else in his eyes now. Something which scared her. Why was he looking like that? And why had his face gone so white? Following the direction of his gaze, she saw the shocking scarlet contrast of blood as it began to drip onto the polished gleam of the wooden floorboards.

And that must have been when she passed out.

CHAPTER TWELVE

ALEK FELT THE clench of pain around his heart—icy-cold and constricting. He couldn't breathe. He couldn't think. He was powerless to help her and even if he'd been capable of helping her—it seemed he wasn't going to get the chance to try. Ellie didn't want him in the ambulance with her, or so one of the paramedics told him, a faintly embarrassed look on his face as he didn't quite dare look him in the eye.

For the first time in his adult life, Alek discovered the feeling of powerlessness. He couldn't insist on doing things *his* way, or overrule what was happening by the sheer force of his personality or financial clout. He was being forced to accept the bitter facts. That Ellie was sick and their baby's life was in danger. That she was being rushed through the London streets with blue lights flashing and sirens blaring and she didn't want him anywhere near her.

A bitter taste stained his mouth.

Who could blame her?

He drove to the hospital as quickly as he could but his usual unerring sense of direction failed him and he found himself lost in the maze of hospital corridors, until a kindly nurse took pity on him and showed him the way to the unit. His heart was in his mouth as he approached that white and sterile place. And still they wouldn't let him see her.

'But I'm her husband,' he said, wondering if the words sounded as fake as they felt. What right did he have to call himself her husband? Was that why the ward sister was fixing him with a disapproving look? Had Ellie blurted out the truth to her in a moment of weakness, begging the nurses not to allow him anywhere near her—this man who had brought her nothing but pain?

'The doctor is with her right now.'

'Please...' His voice broke. It sounded cracked and hollow. Not like his voice at all. But then he'd never asked anyone for anything, had he? Not since those air-conditioned nights in his father's miserable fortress of a house, when he'd lain awake, the pillow clasped tightly over his head but too scared to cry. To the background sound of the night herons which had called across the island, he had silently begged an uncaring god to bring his mother back to him. And then, just like now, events had been completely outside his control. Things didn't happen just because you wanted them to. He saw now that maybe the reason he'd always turned his back on relationships was because, ultimately, he was unable to control them and that control had become his security in an uncertain world. His heart slammed against his ribcage. Or maybe it was just because, until Ellie, he'd never had a real relationship with anyone.

He looked into the ward sister's eyes. 'How is she?'

'She's being stabilised right now.'

'And...the baby?'

His voice cracked again. He hadn't expected

that question to hurt so much, nor for it to mean as much as it did. When had been the critical moment that this unborn life had crept into his heart and taken residence there? The world seemed to tip on its axis as the woman's face assumed an expression of careful calm—as if she was attempting to reassure him without raising false hopes. He guessed she must have been asked that question a million times before.

'I'm afraid it's too early to say.'

He could do nothing but accept her words and he nodded grimly as he was shown into a waiting room which looked onto an ugly brick wall. There was a stack of old magazines on a chipped table and—all too poignantly—a little heap of plastic bricks piled in one corner, presumably for any accompanying children to play with.

Children.

He hadn't wanted any of his own—that had always been a given. He hadn't wanted to risk any child of his having to go through what he had gone through. But now, suddenly, he wanted this baby so bad. He wanted to nurture the child that the baby would grow into.

I will never abandon my baby or hurt or punish him, he thought fiercely. *He will know nothing but love from me—even if I have to learn how to love him from scratch.*

He closed his eyes as the minutes ticked by. Someone brought him a cup of coffee in a plastic cup, but it lay untouched in front of him. And when eventually the doctor came into the waiting room with a ward sister beside him—a different one this time—he sprang to his feet and felt the true meaning of fear. His hands were clammy and cold. His heart was pounding in his chest.

'How is she?' he demanded.

'She's fine—a little shocked and a little scared, but she's had a scan—'

'A scan?' For a second he felt confused. He realised that he'd been thinking in Greek instead of English and the word sounded alien to him.

'We needed to check that the pregnancy is still viable, and I'm delighted to tell you that it is.'

'Still *viable*?' he repeated stupidly.

'The baby is fine,' said the medic gently as if he were speaking to a child. 'Your wife has had a slight bleed, which is not uncommon in early pregnancy—but she's going to have to take it easy from now on. That means no more rushing around. No horse riding.' He smiled gently, as if to prepare him for some kind of blow. 'And no sex, I'm afraid.'

They took him to Ellie's room, where she lay on the narrow hospital bed, looking almost as white as the sheets. Her eyes were closed and her pale fringe was damp with sweat, so that her dark, winged eyebrows looked dramatic against her milky brow.

She didn't stir and, mindful of the doctor's words, he sat down noiselessly in the chair beside the bed, his hand reaching out to cover hers. He didn't know how long he sat there for—only that the rest of the world seemed to have retreated. He measured time by the slow drip of the intravenous bag which was hooked up to her arm. And he must have been looking at that when she eventually woke up, because he turned his head to find her grey eyes fixed steadily on him. He tried to read the expression in them, but he could see nothing.

'Hi,' he said.

She didn't answer, just tugged her hand away from his as she tried to sit up, reaching down to touch her belly, her gaze lifting to his in agonised question.

'The baby?'

He nodded. 'It's okay. The baby's fine.'

She made a choked kind of sob as she slumped back against the pillows, her mouth trembling in relief. 'I didn't dream it, then.'

'Dream what?'

'Someone came.' She licked her lips and paused, as if the effort of speaking was too much. 'They were putting something cold on my stomach. Circling it round and round. They said it was going to be okay, but I thought...'

He felt completely inadequate as her words tailed off and he thought: *You have only yourself to blame. If you hadn't pushed her away, if you hadn't tried to impose your own stupid rules, then you would be able to comfort her now. You'd be able take her in your arms and tell her that everything was going to be all right.*

But he couldn't do that, could he? He couldn't make guarantees he couldn't possibly keep. Promises she'd never believe. All he could do was to make sure she had everything she needed.

'Shh,' he said in as gentle a voice as he'd ever used and she shut her eyes tightly closed, as if she couldn't bear to meet his gaze any longer. 'The doctor says you're going to have to take it easy.'

'I know,' she said as tears began to slide from beneath her lashes.

They kept her in overnight and she was discharged into his care the following day. She tried refusing his offer of a wheelchair, telling him that she was perfectly capable of walking to the car.

'They said to take it easy,' she told him tartly. 'Not to spend the next six months behaving like an invalid.'

'I'm not taking any chances,' came his even response, but his tone was underpinned with steel. 'And if you won't get in the wheelchair, then I shall be forced to pick you up and carry you across the car park—which might cause something of a stir. Up to you, Ellie.'

She glowered but made no further protest as he wheeled her to the car, and she didn't say anything else until they were back at the apartment, when he'd sat her down on one of the squashy sofas and made her the ginger tea she loved.

She glanced up as he walked in with the tray. Her expression was steady and very calm. She drew a deep breath. 'So what are you intending to do about your brother?'

His throat constricted. She'd gone straight for the jugular, hadn't she? 'My brother?' he repeated as if it were the first time he'd ever heard that word. As if he hadn't spent the past twenty-four hours trying to purge his mind of its existence. 'It's you and the baby which are on my mind right now.'

'You're avoiding the subject,' she pointed out. 'Which is par for the course for you. But I'm not going to let this drop, Alek. I'm just not. Before

I went into hospital, we discovered something pretty momentous about your—'

'I don't have a brother,' he cut in harshly. 'Understand?'

Frustratedly, she shook her head. 'I understand that you're pig-headed and stubborn! You might not like the journalist, or the message she left—but that doesn't mean it isn't true. Why would she lie?'

He clenched his hands into fists and another wave of powerlessness washed over him, only this he could do something about. 'I'm not prepared to discuss it any further.'

She shrugged, a look of resignation turning her expression stony. 'Have it your own way. And I'm sure you'll understand that I'm no longer prepared to share my bed with you. I'm moving back into my own bedroom.'

Alek flinched. It hurt more than it should have done, even though it came as no big surprise. Yet something made him want to try to hang on to what they had—and briefly he wondered whether it was a fear of losing her, or just a fear of losing. 'I know the doctor advised no sex, but I can live with that,' he said. 'But that doesn't mean we can't sleep together. I can be there for you in the night if you need anything.'

She stared at him as if he'd taken leave of his senses. 'I can call you if I *need* anything, Alek.'

'But—'

'The charade is over Alek,' she said. 'I'm not sleeping with a stranger any more.'

He looked at her in disbelief. 'How can we possibly be strangers, when you know more about me than anyone else?'

'I only know because I wore you down until you told me—and it was like getting blood from a stone. And I understand why. I realise how painful it was for you to tell me, and that what happened to you is the reason you don't do intimacy. I get all that. But I've also realised that I *want* intimacy. Actually, I crave it. And I can't do sex for sex's sake. I can't do cuddling up together at night-time either. It's too confusing. It blurs the boundaries. It will make me start thinking we're getting closer, but of course we won't be and we never will.'

'Ellie—'

'No,' she said firmly. 'It's important that I say this, so hear me out. I don't blame you for your attitude. I understand why you are the way you are. I think I can almost understand why you don't want to stir up all the emotional stuff of re-uniting with the brother you say you don't have—I just can't live with it. If I were one hundred per cent fit, I think I'd be able to get you to change your mind about wanting to stay with me until after the baby is born. Because I think we both recognise that's no longer really important, and I hope you know me well enough to realise that I'll give you as much contact with your child as you want.' She gave a sad sort of smile, like someone waving goodbye to a ship they knew they would never see again. 'Ideally, I'd like to go back to the New Forest and find myself a little cottage there and live a simple life and look after myself. But obviously I can't do that, because the doctors won't let me and because you're based in London.'

'Ellie—'

'No. Please. Let me finish. I want you to know that I'm grateful to be here and to know you're looking out for me and the baby, because this is all about the baby now. And only the baby.' Her voice was trembling now. 'Because I don't ever want to get physically close to you again, Alek. I can't risk all the fallout and the potential heartbreak. Do you understand?'

And the terrible thing was that he did. He agreed with every reasoned word she'd said. He accepted each hurtful point she made, even though something unfamiliar was bubbling inside him which was urging him to challenge her. To talk her round.

But he couldn't. One of the reasons for his outstanding achievements in the world of commerce was an ability to see things as they really were. His vision was X-ray clear whenever he looked at a run-down business, with the intention of turning it around to make a profit. And he realised that he must apply the same kind of logic now. It was what it was. He had destroyed any kind of future with the mother of his child and he must live with her decision and accept it. She was better off without someone like him, anyway. A man who couldn't do feelings. Who was too afraid to try.

A pain like a cold and remorseless wind swept through him.

'Yes, I understand,' he said.

CHAPTER THIRTEEN

So why was he so damned restless?

Alek stared out of his office window and drummed his fingers impatiently on his desk. Why couldn't he accept a life which—despite having a pregnant wife living in his apartment— was still tailored to fit his needs? He told himself that things weren't *really* that different. Why should it bother him so much that he and Ellie were now back in separate rooms?

He still went to work each morning just the way he'd always done, although Ellie had taken to sleeping late these days instead of joining him for tea before he went to the office. At least, he was assuming she was sleeping. She might have been wide awake, doing naked yoga moves as the sun rose for all he knew. Or submerging her rapidly growing bump beneath a bath filled to the brim with sensual bubbles. He had no idea what went on behind her bedroom door once it was closed, although he'd fantasised about it often enough. Hell, yes.

He wondered if his frustration showed in his face. Whether he'd given himself away the other morning, when he'd unexpectedly seen her padding back from the kitchen clutching a mug of ginger tea as he'd been about to take an early morning conference call. Her hair had been tumbling in glorious disarray around her shoulders and the floaty, flowery robe she wore had managed to conceal her changing shape while somehow emphasising it. Her skin had been fresh and her eyes bright, despite the earliness of the hour. She'd looked more like a teenager than a woman of twenty-five and he'd felt a pang of something like regret. Just the day before, the doctor had given her a glowing bill of health. Mother and baby were ticking all the right boxes, and Alek told himself that at least something good had come out of all this.

But wasn't it funny how you always wanted

what you hadn't got? Why else would he be craving more of her company and wishing she'd linger longer over dinner? Wanting her to say something—anything—other than make those polite little observations about what kind of day she'd had. He'd made quite a few concessions to fit in with her pregnancy, but even they hadn't softened her resolve. Hadn't he eaten his words and joined that wretched antenatal class, where they were expected to lie on the floor—puffing like a bunch of whales? Yet still she kept her distance. He felt a stab of conscience. Wasn't that how he used to be with her? And wasn't he discovering that he didn't much like being pushed away? And in the meantime, he was aching for her. Aching in ways which were nothing to do with sex.

He'd been brooding about it all week and not coming up with any answers about how he could change things, when on Saturday night she looked at him across the dinner table with an odd expression on her face.

'I want you to know,' she said in the careful

way people did when they'd been practising say-ing something, 'that if you decide you want to start seeing other…women, I shan't mind.'

His fork fell to his plate with a clatter. His heart pounded. Rarely had he been more shocked. Or outraged. 'Say that again,' he breathed.

'You heard me perfectly well, Alek. I'm just asking you to be discreet about it, that's all. I don't particularly want—'

'No, wait a minute.' Ruthlessly he cut across her words in a way he'd avoided doing of late, leaning across the table and glaring at her. 'Are you telling me that you *want* me to start dating other women?'

Ellie didn't reply, not immediately. She fiddled around with her napkin for just long enough to hang on to her composure—telling herself that this was the only solution. She couldn't keep him chained up like a tame lion. 'I don't know if *want* is the right word—'

'Maybe you want to watch?' he suggested crudely. 'Perhaps that's one of your fantasises.'

Does the thought of me having sex with some-body else turn you on, Ellie?'

'Don't be so disgusting!' she snapped, feeling her cheeks growing hot. 'That's not what I meant at all and you know it.'

'Do I?' he demanded furiously. 'What am I supposed to think, when you give me your bless-ing to have sex with someone else, while you're still living under my roof?'

She glared back. 'I wasn't giving you my *bless-ing*. I'm trying to be fair!'

'Fair?' he echoed, furiously.

'Yes, fair.' She took a shaky sip of water. 'I know you're a virile man with a healthy sexual appetite and I shouldn't expect you to have to curtail that, just because...'

'Because you no longer want me?'

Ellie swallowed as she met the accusation spit-ting from his blue eyes. Oh, if only. If only it were as simple as that. 'It's not that I don't want you.'

'You just take masochistic pleasure in us sleeping apart? In me lying wide-eyed for most of the night knowing you're in the room next door?'

'I told you before. I can't do fake intimacy. And I didn't start this conversation to discuss the reasons why I won't sleep with you.'

'Then why *did* you start it?'

'Because I'm trying to be kind.'

'Kind?' He stared at her incredulously. 'How does that work?'

'I'm just suggesting that if you want to relieve your frustrations, then feel free—but please be discreet about it. I just don't want it in my face, that's all.'

There was silence for a moment while he stared down at his clenched fists and when he looked up again, there was something in his eyes she didn't recognise.

'Why not you?' he questioned simply. 'When you're the only woman I want? When we both know that if I came round to the other side of that table and started kissing you, you'd go up in flames—the way you always do when I touch you.'

'So why don't you?' she challenged. 'Why don't you take control, as you're so good at doing? Take the choice away from me?'

He shook his head and gave a short laugh. 'Because that would make it too easy. A short-term fix, not a long-term solution. You have to be with me because you want to, Ellie—and not just because your body is reacting to something I do to you.'

She stared at her napkin. She stared at her water glass. But when she looked up, she shook her head. 'I can't,' she said. 'It would be insane to even try. We're planning a divorce before too long and I want to acclimatise myself to the situation. I'm trying to get used to the separate lives we've agreed to lead.'

For a minute there was silence.

'And what if I told you I don't want separate lives, or a divorce?' he said at last. 'That I wanted to start over, only this time to do it differently? We'll take it as slow as you like, Ellie. I'll court you, if that's what you want. I'll woo you with flowers. I won't take business calls when we're away. I'll do whatever it takes, if you just give me another chance.'

His bright eyes bored into her and for a moment Ellie couldn't speak, because she got the feeling that Alek didn't often ask questions like that. And hadn't she sometimes dreamt of a moment like this—even though she'd told herself it would never happen? But it *was* happening. He was sitting there and saying things she'd longed to hear and temptation was tugging at her—because Alek in a peace-making mood was pretty irresistible. His blue eyes were blazing and his lips were parted, as if already anticipating her kiss—and didn't she want to kiss him so badly? She could go into his arms and they could just lose themselves in each other, and...

And what?

How long before domesticity bored him? Before the emotional demands *she would inevitably make* became too tedious for him to bear? Because he still didn't do communication, did he? Not about the things that really mattered. He was still denying that he had a brother. He was only talking this way because he was bargaining with her. Because it was probably frustrating the life out of him that she wasn't falling into his arms with gratitude.

She shook her head. 'I can't.'

'Why not?'

She realised that his pride was going to be hurt—and maybe that wasn't a bad thing. But she needed to show him that this was about more than pride. She had to summon up enough courage and strength to present him with a few harsh home truths.

'Because I can't contemplate life with a man who keeps running away.'

'Running away?' he echoed and she heard the anger building in his voice. 'Are you accusing me of cowardice, Ellie?'

'It's up to you to make the diagnosis, not me.' She stared at the little vase of blue flowers which sat at the centre of the table. She thought how delicate the petals were. How most things in life were delicate, when you stopped to think about it. She lifted her gaze to his, trying not to react to his anger. 'When you told me all about your family—about your mother walking out on you and the effect it had on you—I could understand why you never tried to get in touch with her. I understood that you'd taken your pain and turned it into success and that it was easier to turn your back on the past. But you're an adult now, with the world at your fingertips—the most success-ful man I've ever met. You're intelligent and re-sourceful and yet you've just heard that you've got a brother and you're acting like nothing's hap-pened!'

His dark head was bent and there was silence, and when at last he looked at her she flinched from the pain she saw written in his eyes.

'Not just a brother,' he said. 'I think I could have dealt with that. But a twin brother? Do you know what that means, if it's true? Have you thought about it, Ellie? She didn't have another baby with another man. She had one who was exactly the same age. *She took him with her and left me behind.* I was the one she rejected. I was the one she didn't want. How do you think that makes me feel?'

'I don't think it makes you *feel* anything,' she whispered back. 'Because you're blocking out your feelings, the way you've always done. You're ignoring it and pretending it isn't there and hoping it will go away. But it won't go away. It will just fester and fester and make you bitter. And I don't want a man like that. I want someone who can face up to reality. Who can accept how it's making him feel—even if it hurts—and who isn't afraid to show it.'

She leant forward and her voice was fervent. 'The stuff you imagine is always worse than the real thing,' she said. 'I know that. When I met my father—all the dreams I'd nurtured about us becoming one big happy family were destroyed the moment he pushed the table away and my cappuccino spilt everywhere. And of course I was upset. But afterwards I felt...well, free, I suppose. I could let go of all those foolish fantasies. Because it's better to deal with reality, than with dreams. Or nightmares,' she finished as she rose to her feet. She looked into his face and saw the pain which was written there. Such raw and bitter pain that it made her instinctively want to reach out and comfort him.

But she knew she couldn't rid him of his nightmares. She couldn't *fix* Alek. He had to do that all by himself.

CHAPTER FOURTEEN

HE DIDN'T TELL her he was leaving until the morning of his departure, when Ellie walked into the kitchen and saw him drinking coffee, a leather bag on the floor beside his feet. He turned as she entered the room and, although his hooded eyes gave nothing away, his powerful body was stiff with tension. A trickle of apprehension began to whisper down her spine.

'You're going away on a business trip?' she questioned.

He shook his head. 'I'm going to Paris.'

Fear and dread punched at her heart in rapid succession. Paris. The city of romance. She looked down. An overnight bag. The fear grew. 'You've decided to take me up on my offer?' she breathed in horror.

He frowned. 'What offer?'

'You're seeing someone else?'

His brow darkened. She saw a pulse flicker at his temple. 'Are you crazy? I'm going to meet my brother. I phoned the journalist and spoke to her. She gave me his details and I emailed him. We're having lunch at the Paris Ritz later.'

Ellie's heart flooded with a complex mixture of emotions. There was relief that he hadn't taken her up on her foolish suggestion and joy that he'd taken the step of arranging to meet his brother. But there was disappointment, too. He was facing up to his demons—but he hadn't stopped to think that she might like to be involved, too. She was curious to meet her baby's uncle, yes—and wasn't it possible she could be a support to her husband if she was there at his side? She took an eager step towards him, but the emphatic shake of his head halted her.

'Please don't,' he said. 'Elaborate displays of emotion are the last thing I want to deal with right now.'

It wasn't an unreasonable reaction in the circumstances, but that didn't stop it from hurting.

Ellie's arms hung uselessly by her sides as she pursed her lips. Yet, why *should* he accept her comfort or her help when she'd spent weeks pushing him away?

She nodded. 'Good luck,' she said quietly, though never had she wanted to kiss him quite so much.

She spent the day trying not to think about what might be happening in France. She told herself that Alek wouldn't ring and she was right. Every time she glanced at her phone—too often—there were no texts or missed calls and the small screen remained infuriatingly blank. She'd been due to meet Alannah for lunch, but she cancelled— afraid she would end up doing something stupid, like crying. Or even worse, that she would blurt out the whole story. And she couldn't do that. It wasn't her story to tell. She'd already broken Alek's confidence once and to do so again—wittingly this time—would be unforgivable.

She tried to keep herself occupied as best she could. There was a subtle nip to the air, so she slipped on a jacket and walked across a park with leaves showing the distinct bronzed brush-strokes of autumn. She went shopping for food in the little deli she'd discovered, which was hidden unexpectedly in a narrow road behind the smart Knightsbridge shops, and she bought all the things she knew Alek liked best to eat.

But no matter what she did, she couldn't clear her mind of nagging questions which couldn't be answered until he arrived home. Though it occurred to her at some point that he might not want to tell her anything. He was naturally secretive and that wouldn't necessarily have changed. Discovering something about his past wasn't necessarily going to transform him into someone who was comfortable with disclosure.

She went to bed at around eleven and it was sometime later that she heard the sound of a key in the lock and a door quietly closing. Her throat dried. He was home. She could hear him moving around, as if he didn't want to wake her, but as the footsteps passed her door she called out to him.

'Alek.'

The footsteps halted. The floor creaked and there was silence.

'Alek?' she said again.

The door opened and a powerful shaft of light slanted across the room to shine on her bed, like a spotlight. She blinked a little in the fierce gleam and sat up, pushing her hair out of her eyes. She tried to search his face, but his eyes were in shadow and all she could see was his powerful body silhouetted against the bright light.

'Are you okay?' she said.

'I didn't want to wake you.'

'Won't you...come in?' Her voice gave a nervous wobble as she switched on the bedside lamp. 'And tell me what happened.'

She'd been half expecting him to refuse, to coolly inform her that he'd tell her everything— well, maybe not quite everything—in the morning. That would be much more characteristic of the Alek she knew. But he didn't. He walked into the room and sat down on the edge of the bed, only she noticed he kept his distance—as if ensuring that he was nowhere within touching range. And stupidly—because it wasn't very appropriate in the circumstances—she found herself wishing she were wearing some provocative little excuse for a nightie, instead of an oversized T-shirt which had nothing but comfort to commend it.

'So,' she said nervously. 'What happened?'

Alek looked at the way she was biting her lip. At the shiny hair spilling over her shoulders and the anxiousness she couldn't quite keep from her eyes. He thought that she loved him, but he couldn't be sure. His mouth hardened. How could you tell if a woman really loved you? He had no baseline to work from.

'We met,' he said. 'And after a while he showed me some photos. The first—' His voice cracked slightly. 'The first photos I'd ever seen of her.'

She nodded. Swallowed. 'What were they like?'

He tipped his head and looked up at the ceiling. 'She was very beautiful—even in the later shots. She had this thick black hair and the most amazing blue eyes.'

'Like yours, you mean?'

He gave a wry smile as he looked at her again. 'That's right. Just like mine.' It had been beyond strange to see the physical evidence of somebody he'd only ever heard about in the most negative terms. A woman in a cotton dress, glinting at the sun—her face filled with an unmistakable sadness.

'And what was your brother like?'

Ellie's words broke into his thoughts and Alek opened his mouth to answer but the most articulate person in the world would've had difficulty expressing the conflicting feelings which had torn through him when he'd seen his twin brother for the first time.

'He looks like me,' he said, at last.

'Your twin brother looks like you? You don't say!'

And unexpectedly, he began to laugh—her quip doing the impossible and taking some of the heat out of the situation. He thought about how he'd felt when he'd walked into the famous hotel and seen a black-haired man with a face so scarily like his own, staring back at him from the other side of the restaurant. He remembered the over-powering sense of recognition which had rocked him and momentarily robbed him of breath.

'His name is Loukas but his eyes are black,' he said. 'Not blue.'

And that had been the only physical difference he'd been able to see, although after the second bottle of wine Loukas had told him about the scars which tracked over his back, and what had caused them. He'd told him a lot of stuff. Some of which was hard to hear. Some he'd wanted instantly to forget. About a mother who had been a congenitally bad picker of men, and the sorry way that had influenced her life. About his poverty-stricken childhood—so different from Alek's, but not without its own problems. Dark problems which Loukas had told him he would save for another day.

'Had he been trying to find you for a long time?' Ellie whispered.

He shook his head. 'He only discovered that I existed last year, when his...our...mother died.'

'Oh, Alek.'

He shook his head, unprepared for the rush of emotion, wanting to stem it, in case it made him do what he'd been trying very hard not to do all day. He cleared his throat and concentrated on the facts.

'She left behind a long letter, explaining why she'd done what she'd done. She said she knew she couldn't live with my father any more—that his rages and infidelities were becoming intolerable. She had no money and no power—she was essentially trapped on his island. She thought he would blight the lives of all three of us if she stayed, but she also knew that there was no way she could cope with two babies. And so she… she chose Loukas.'

She nodded, not saying anything and for a moment he thought she wasn't going to ask it, but of course she asked it. This was Ellie, after all.

'How did she choose?'

Another silence. 'She tossed a coin.'

'Oh.' Her voice was very quiet. 'Oh, I see.'

He gave a bitter laugh. He wasn't a man given to flights of fancy but he'd vividly imagined that moment just before she'd walked out of the house for good. He'd wanted his brother to lie; to invent a fairy story. To tell him that she'd chosen Loukas because he had been weaker, or because she thought that Alek would fare better because he was two minutes older and a pound heavier. Or because Loukas had cried at the last minute and it had torn at her heartstrings. But no. It was something much more prosaic than that. His fate and the fate of his brother being decided by a coin spinning in the air, until it landed on the back of her hand and she covered it with her palm. What had she thought as she'd lifted her hand to see which boy would be going with her, and which boy would be left behind? Did she find it easy to walk away from him?

'My mother flipped a coin and I lost out,' he said.

Another silence. A much longer one this time.

'You know she did it because she loved you?' she said suddenly. 'You do realise that?'

He raised his head, barely noticing the salty

prickling at the backs of his eyes. 'What the hell are you talking about?'

'She did it because she loved you,' she repeated, more fiercely. 'She must have done. She must have been out of her head with worry—knowing that she could barely look after one baby, let alone two. And if she'd taken you both, he would have come after you. He definitely would. She must have thought your father would be glad to have been left with one son, and that he'd love you as best he could. But he couldn't. He just couldn't—for reasons you'll probably never know. But what you have to do, is to stop thinking that because of what happened you're unlovable—because you aren't. You need to accept that you're very lovable indeed, if only you'd stop shutting people out. Our baby is going to love you, that's for sure. And I've got so much love in my heart that I'm bursting to give you—if only you'll let me. Oh, darling. Darling. It's all right. It's all right. Oh, Alek—come here.' Her eyes began to blur. 'Everything's going to be all right.'

She put her arms around him and he did what

he'd been trying not to do all day, which was to cry. He cried the tears he'd never cried before. Tears of loneliness and pain, which eventually gave way to the realisation that he was free at last. Free of the past and all its dark tentacles. He had let it go and Ellie had helped him do that.

His hand was shaking as he smoothed the pale hair away from her face and looked at her.

'You would never do that,' he said.

She turned her head slightly, so that she could kiss the hand which was still cupping the side of her face. 'Do what?'

'Leave our baby.'

She turned her head back, biting her lip, her grey eyes darkening. 'I don't want to judge your mother, or to compare—'

'That wasn't my aim,' he said quietly. 'I'm just stating a fact and letting myself be grateful for that fact. I've given you a hard time, Ellie, and a lot of women might have lost patience with me before now. Yet you didn't. You hung on in there. You gave me strength and showed me the way.'

His question shimmered on the air as she looked into his eyes.

'Because I love you,' she said simply. 'You must have realised that by now? But love sometimes means having to take a step back, because it can never flourish if there are darknesses or secrets, or things which never dare be spoken about.'

'And I love you,' he said, his free hand reaching out to lie possessively over the bump of their un-born child. A lump rose in his throat as he felt the powerful ripple of movement beneath. 'I love you and our baby and I will love you both for ever. I will nurture and care for you both and never let you down. Be very certain of that, *poulaki mou*. I will never let you down.'

He could taste the salt from her own tears as he kissed her and did what he'd been wanting to do for so long. He lay down beside her and put his arms around her, gathering her close against his beating heart.

EPILOGUE

'SO WHAT'S IT LIKE, being back?' Ellie's words seemed to float through the warm night air towards her husband. 'Is it weird?'

Shining brightly through the unshuttered windows, the moon had turned the room into a fantasy setting of indigo and silver. Over their heads whirled a big old-fashioned fan and the sheets were rumpled around their gleaming bodies. The faint scent of sex hung in the air and mingled with the tang of the lemons squeezed into the water jug which stood beside the bed.

Ellie turned onto her side and looked at Alek, who lay beside her with his arms stretched above his head, looking a picture of blissful contentment.

This journey to Kristalothos was one they'd waited a while to make, until both of them were certain they were ready. A trip to the island home of Alek's childhood—a place which symbolised so much of the darkness and horror of his past— was never going to be at the top of their bucket list. In fact, Ellie had been surprised when Alek had first suggested it because although their life had been hectic, it was pretty close to perfect. The birth of their son two years previously had put the seal on their happiness and Ellie had been...

She swallowed.

Frightened that going back would test their happiness and threaten to destroy it? Scared he might go back to being the secretive Alek of old who had locked her out of his heart—or that the reality of confronting his past might bring renewed bitterness?

Yes, she had thought all those things—and more. But she'd quashed her fears and entered into his plans with enthusiasm, because she'd sensed it was something he'd needed to do. Hadn't she been the one who'd insisted you had to face your fears instead of running away from them? And perhaps there was some truth in the idea that you could never go forward until you were properly at peace with your past.

After much discussion, they had decided to leave their little boy behind in England. Young Loukas—their adored son, who they'd named after Alek's twin brother and who had given them so much more than joy. It was the tiny tot more than anything who had been responsible for Alek's growing ability to show emotion. Because children loved unconditionally and Alek had learnt to do the same. He had learnt that real love knew no boundaries and sometimes Ellie just sat watching him play with their little boy and her heart swelled up with so much pride and affection.

But a lively two-year-old was not an ideal companion for a cathartic trip which might be emotionally painful, which was why they'd left him behind with Bridget—who had become his honorary grandmother.

Ellie and Alek had chartered a boat from Athens, which had taken them out to his childhood island home of Kristalothos, with the vessel making a foamy trail through the wine-dark sea as they journeyed. They had arrived on a spring morning, when the wild flowers were massed over the gentle hills and the sea was crystal clear as it lapped gently against the fine white sand.

As he had looked around him with slightly dazed eyes, Alek had told her the place had changed beyond recognition. Some of the changes he'd discovered when he was making plans for their trip but seeing them with his own eyes had really driven home the fact that nothing ever stayed the same. A Greek-born hotelier named Zak Constantides had bought his father's old fortress and razed it to the ground, putting in its place a boutique hotel, which was fast becoming as famous as his iconic London Granchester.

But Alek had chosen to rent a villa instead of staying there and Ellie was glad, because she didn't want to spend a single night on the spot where a young boy had spent so many miserable years.

She leant across the rumpled bed and stroked

her fingertips over his bronzed cheek, and her touch seemed to stir him from his pensive mood. He smiled as he reached for her and thought about her question.

What was it like being back?

Reflectively, he stroked her hair. 'It is a bit weird,' he admitted. 'But it doesn't hurt. Not any more. And I'm glad I came, because it was something I needed to do. Another ghost laid to rest. I like the fact that Zak's hotel has brought work and prosperity to the island and that the place is no longer ruled by fear and oppression.'

'I'm glad, too,' she said, wriggling up closer.

'But I'm glad of so many things,' he said. 'Mainly for my beautiful wife and my equally beautiful son, who provide me with the kind of contentment I never thought existed.' He tilted her chin with the tip of his finger, so he could see the gleam of her eyes in the moonlight. 'I'm even glad that I've got a brother, although—'

'Although Loukas has his own demons,' she finished slowly.

'Yes, he does. But it isn't Loukas I'm thinking

about at this moment, *poulaki mou*. It's you.' He rolled on top of her, his fingers playing with the tumble of her hair as he felt the softness of her body beneath him. 'Because without you I would have nothing. I am who I am because of you, Ellie. You made me confront things I'd spent my life avoiding. You made me look at myself, even though I didn't want to. I've learnt...'

'What have you learnt?' she questioned softly as his voice tailed off.

He shrugged. 'That it's better to face up to the truth rather than to block it out. And that feelings don't kill you—even the very toughest ones. Everything that's worth knowing, you have taught me and I love you for that, Ellie Sarantos—and for a million reasons more besides.' He gave a mock glower of a frown. 'Even though you have stubbornly refused to let me announce that particular piece of information to the world.'

He traced a thoughtful finger over the angled line of her collarbone. He had wanted to go through a second marriage ceremony—a big glitzy occasion at the Greek Cathedral in

London, intended as a mark of his love for her because he felt she'd been short-changed last time. For a while Ellie had been agreeable—even consulting a wedding planner and hearing about the rival merits of a string quartet versus an old-fashioned bouzouki band for the reception. Until one morning at breakfast, she'd told him she didn't need declarations or lavish gestures. That it was enough to know he cared, and in the private moments of their precious relationship his heartfelt words of love meant more than a truckload of confetti.

And wasn't that another aspect of her personality which made him love her so much? That the things she cared about weren't the *things* which so many people strived for. She didn't need to put on a show or make some kind of statement. She didn't need to prove anything. Diamonds she could take or leave, and, although she wore silky tea dresses because she knew he liked them, she was happiest in a pair of jeans and a T-shirt. She was still Ellie—the same straightforward, uncomplicated woman he'd first fallen for—and he wouldn't want her any other way.

He reached for her breasts and cupped them and she made a purring little sound in the back of her throat, because she liked it. *Theos*, but he liked it, too. But then he liked everything about his soft and beautiful wife.

'Shall I make love to you now?' he questioned.

She touched her fingertips to the dark shadow of his jaw and followed it up with the slow drift of her lips. 'Oh, yes, please,' she whispered.

They were in the place of his birth, but they could have been anywhere. A place which had once symbolised darkness and heartbreak, but not any more. Because Ellie made everywhere feel like the home he'd never really had. Ellie breathed life into *his* life. He bent his head and kissed her as the night herons gathered around the lapping bay outside their window.

* * * * *

Leabharlanna Poiblí Chathair Baile Átha Cliath

Dublin City Public Libraries

MILLS & BOON®
Large Print – August 2015

THE BILLIONAIRE'S BRIDAL BARGAIN
Lynne Graham

AT THE BRAZILIAN'S COMMAND
Susan Stephens

CARRYING THE GREEK'S HEIR
Sharon Kendrick

THE SHEIKH'S PRINCESS BRIDE
Annie West

HIS DIAMOND OF CONVENIENCE
Maisey Yates

OLIVERO'S OUTRAGEOUS PROPOSAL
Kate Walker

THE ITALIAN'S DEAL FOR I DO
Jennifer Hayward

THE MILLIONAIRE AND THE MAID
Michelle Douglas

EXPECTING THE EARL'S BABY
Jessica Gilmore

BEST MAN FOR THE BRIDESMAID
Jennifer Faye

IT STARTED AT A WEDDING...
Kate Hardy

MILLS & BOON®
Large Print – September 2015

THE SHEIKH'S SECRET BABIES
Lynne Graham

THE SINS OF SEBASTIAN REY-DEFOE
Kim Lawrence

AT HER BOSS'S PLEASURE
Cathy Williams

CAPTIVE OF KADAR
Trish Morey

THE MARAKAIOS MARRIAGE
Kate Hewitt

CRAVING HER ENEMY'S TOUCH
Rachael Thomas

THE GREEK'S PREGNANT BRIDE
Michelle Smart

THE PREGNANCY SECRET
Cara Colter

A BRIDE FOR THE RUNAWAY GROOM
Scarlet Wilson

THE WEDDING PLANNER AND THE CEO
Alison Roberts

BOUND BY A BABY BUMP
Ellie Darkins

MILLS & BOON®

Why shop at millsandboon.co.uk?

Each year, thousands of romance readers find their perfect read at millsandboon.co.uk. That's because we're passionate about bringing you the very best romantic fiction. Here are some of the advantages of shopping at www.millsandboon.co.uk:

* **Get new books first**—you'll be able to buy your favourite books one month before they hit the shops

* **Get exclusive discounts**—you'll also be able to buy our specially created monthly collections, with up to 50% off the RRP

* **Find your favourite authors**—latest news, interviews and new releases for all your favourite authors and series on our website, plus ideas for what to try next

* **Join in**—once you've bought your favourite books, don't forget to register with us to rate, review and join in the discussions

Visit **www.millsandboon.co.uk**
for all this and more today!

MILLS_WEB_LP